THE GHOST STORIES OF MURIEL SPARK

THE GHOST STORIES OF MURIEL SPARK

A NEW DIRECTIONS BOOK

Publisher's Note: These eight ghost stories are taken from New Directions *All the Stories of Muriel Spark* and published by arrangement with the author and her agent, George Borchardt, Inc., New York.

Grateful acknowledgments are made to the editors and publishers of the magazines in which these stories first appeared:
"The House of the Famous Poet," "The Executor," "Another Pair of Hands," and "The Hanging Judge," first appeared in *The New Yorker*:
Others appeared in *Botteghe Obscure, Ellery Queen Mystery Magazine, The London Mystery Magazine*, and *The Observer*.

Manufactured in the United States of America.
New Directions Books are printed on acid-free paper.
First published as a New Directions Paperbook (NDP963) in 2003.

Library of Congress Cataloging-in-Publication Data
Spark, Muriel.
  The ghost stories of Muriel Spark.
    p. cm.
  ISBN 0-8112-1549-0 (alk. paper)
  1. Ghost stories, Scottish. I. Title.
PR6037.P29A6 2003
823'.914—dc22   2003014485

New Directions Books are published for James Laughlin
by New Directions Publishing Corporation,
80 Eighth Avenue, New York 10011

CONTENTS

THE GHOST STORIES OF

MURIEL SPARK

THE GIRL I LEFT
BEHIND ME

IT WAS JUST GONE quarter past six when I
left the office.

"Teedle-um-tum-tum"—there was the tune
again, going round my head. Mr. Letter had been
whistling it all throughout the day between his
noisy telephone calls and his dreamy sessions.
Sometimes he whistled "Softly, Softly, Turn the
Key," but usually it was "The Girl I Left Behind
Me" rendered at a brisk hornpipe tempo.

I stood in the bus line, tired out, and wondering how long I would endure Mark Letter (Screws
& Nails) Ltd. Of course, after my long illness, it
was experience. But Mr. Letter and his tune, and
his sudden moods of bounce, and his sudden
lapses into lassitude, his sandy hair and little bad

teeth, roused my resentment, especially when his tune barrelled round my head long after I had left the office; it was like taking Mr. Letter home.

No one at the bus stop took any notice of me. Well, of course, why should they? I was not acquainted with anyone there, but that evening I felt particularly anonymous among the homegoers. Everyone looked right through me and even, it seemed, walked through me. Late autumn always sets my fancy toward sad ideas. The starlings were crowding in to roost on all the high cornices of the great office buildings. And I located, among the misty unease of my feelings, a very strong conviction that I had left something important behind me or some job incompleted at the office. Perhaps I had left the safe unlocked, or perhaps it was something quite trivial which nagged at me. I had half a mind to turn back, tired as I was, and reassure myself. But my bus came along and I piled in with the rest.

As usual, I did not get a seat. I clung to the handrail and allowed myself to be lurched back and forth against the other passengers. I stood on a man's foot, and said, "Oh, sorry." But he looked away without response, which depressed me. And more and more, I felt that I had left something of tremendous import at the office. "Teedle-um-tum-tum"—the tune was a background to my worry all the way home. I went over in my mind the day's business, for I thought, now, perhaps it was a letter which I should have written and posted on my way home.

That morning I had arrived at the office to find Mark Letter vigorously at work. By fits, he would occasionally turn up at eight in the morning, tear at the post and, by the time I arrived, he would have despatched perhaps half a dozen needless telegrams; and before I could get my coat off, would deliver a whole day's instructions to me, rapidly fluttering his freckled hands in time with his chattering mouth. This habit used to jar me, and I found only one thing amusing about it; that was when he would say, as he gave instructions for dealing with each item, "Mark letter urgent." I thought that rather funny coming from Mark Letter, and I often thought of him, as he was in those moods, as Mark Letter Urgent.

As I swayed in the bus I recalled that morning's access of energy on the part of Mark Letter Urgent. He had been more urgent than usual, so that I still felt put out by the urgency. I felt terribly old for my twenty-two years as I raked round my mind for some clue as to what I had left unfinished. Something had been left amiss; the further the bus carried me from the office, the more certain I became of it. Not that I took my job to heart very greatly, but Mr. Letter's moods of bustle were infectious, and when they occurred I felt fussy for the rest of the day; and although I consoled myself that I would feel better when I got home, the worry would not leave me.

By noon, Mr. Letter had calmed down a little, and for an hour before I went to lunch he strode round the office with his hands in his pockets, whistling between his seedy brown teeth that sailors' song "The Girl I Left Behind Me." I lurched with the bus as it chugged out the rhythm, "Teedle-um-tum-tum. Teedle-um . . ." Returning from lunch I had found silence, and wondered if Mr. Letter was out, until I heard suddenly, from his tiny private office, his tune again, a low swift hum, trailing out toward the end. Then I knew that he had fallen into one of his afternoon daydreams.

I would sometimes come upon him in his little box of an office when these trances afflicted him. I would find him sitting in his swivel chair behind his desk. Usually he had taken off his coat and slung it across the back of his chair. His right elbow would be propped on the desk, supporting his chin, while from his left hand would dangle his tie. He would gaze at this tie; it was his main object of contemplation. That afternoon I had found him tie-gazing when I went into his room for some papers. He was gazing at it with parted lips so that I could see his small, separated discolored teeth, no larger than a child's first teeth. Through them he whistled his tune. Yesterday, it had been "Softly, Softly, Turn the Key," but today it was the other.

I got off the bus at my usual stop, with my fare still in my hand. I almost threw the coins away, absentmindedly thinking they were the ticket, and when I noticed them I thought how nearly no one at all I was, since even the conductor had, in his rush, passed me by.

Mark Letter had remained in his dream for two and a half hours. What was it I had left unfinished? I could not for the life of me recall what he had said when at last he emerged from his office-box. Perhaps it was then I had made tea. Mr. Letter always liked a cup when he was neither in his frenzy nor in his abstraction, but ordinary and talkative. He would speak of his hobby, fretwork. I do not think Mr. Letter had any home life. At forty-six he was still unmarried, living alone in a house at Roehampton. As I walked up the lane to my lodgings I recollected that Mr. Letter had come in for his tea with his tie still dangling from his hand, his throat white under the open-neck shirt, and his "Teedle-um-tum-tum" in his teeth.

At last I was home and my Yale in the lock. Softly, I said to myself, softly turn the key, and thank God I'm home. My landlady passed through the hall from kitchen to dining-room with a salt and pepper cruet in her crinkly hands. She had some new lodgers. "My guests," she always called them. The new guests took precedence over the old with my landlady. I felt desolate. I simply could not climb the stairs to my room to wash, and then descend to take brown soup with the new guests while my landlady fussed over them, ignoring me. I sat for a moment in the chair in the hall to collect my strength. A year's illness drains one, however young. Suddenly the repulsion of the brown soup and the anxiety about the office made me decide. I would not go upstairs to my room. I must return to the office to see what it was that I had overlooked.

"Teedle-um-tum-tum"—I told myself that I was giving way to neurosis. Many times I had laughed at my sister who, after she had gone to bed at night, would send her husband downstairs to make sure all the gas taps were turned off, all the doors locked, back and front. Very well, I was as silly as my sister, but I understood her obsession, and simply opened the door and slipped out of the house, tired as I was, making my weary way back to the bus stop, back to the office.

"Why should I do this for Mark Letter?" I demanded of myself. But really, I was not returning for his sake, it was for my own. I was doing this to get rid of the feeling of incompletion, and that song in my brain swimming round like a damned goldfish.

I wondered, as the bus took me back along the familiar route, what I would say if Mark Letter should still be at the office. He often worked late, or at least, stayed there late, doing I don't know what, for his screw and nail business did not call for long hours. It seemed to me he had an affection for those dingy premises. I was rather apprehensive lest I should find Mr. Letter at the office, standing, just as I had last seen him, swinging his tie in his hand, beside my desk. I resolved that if I should find him there, I should say straight out that I had left something behind me.

A clock struck quarter past seven as I got off the bus. I realized that again I had not paid my fare. I looked at the money in my hand for a stupid second. Then I felt reckless. "Teedle-um-tum-tum"—I caught myself humming the tune as I walked quickly up the sad side street to our office. My heart knocked at my throat, for I was eager. Softly, softly, I said to myself as I turned the key of the outside door. Quickly, quickly, I ran up the stairs. Only outside the office door I halted, and while I found its key on my bunch it occurred to me how strangely my sister would think I was behaving.

I opened the door and my sadness left me at once. With a great joy I recognized what it was I had left behind me, my body lying strangled on the floor. I ran toward my body and embraced it like a lover.

THE HANGING JUDGE

"THE PASSING OF sentence," wrote one of the newspapers, "obviously tried the elderly judge. In fact, he looked as if he had seen a ghost." This was not the only comment that drew attention to Sir Sullivan Stanley's expression under his wig and that deadly black cap required by British law at the time. It was the autumn following the lovely summer of 1947. The yellow and brown leaves scuttled merrily along the paths in the park.

It had been Justice Stanley's lot to condemn to death several men in the course of his career—no women, incidentally, but that was due to the extreme rarity of women murderers. Certainly, no one would have suggested that Sullivan Stanley would hesitate in the case of a woman to pronounce the words, like a tolling bell, "that you be taken from this place . . . and that you be there hanged by the neck until you be dead." (And, almost as an afterthought, "May the Lord have mercy on your soul.")

The man in the dock was in his thirties, good-looking, as respectable a person in appearance as might be found briskly crossing the street outside the Old Bailey where the trial was taking place. He was George Forrester, perpetrator of what were known to the radio-listening and newspaper-reading public of those days as "the mud-river murders."

Sir Sullivan Stanley's facial expression throughout the trial had been no different from his expression at any other time or in any other trial. He invariably gave the impression that he was irritated by the accused—especially in one notable case where a man had pleaded guilty and refused to be persuaded by his own counsel or anybody else that "guilty" and "not guilty" were mere technicalities, that in fact to plead guilty dispensed more or less with the trial. In no previous case, then, had the press remarked on this expression. Sir Sullivan had loose, spaniel-like jowls and looked the age he was and as annoyed as he was. But "something seemed to come over the Justice," wrote another reporter. "He was plainly shaken, not so much when he heard the foreman of the jury pronounce the word "guilty" as when he put on the black cap which had been lying before him. Can it be possible," speculated this reporter, "that Judge Stanley is beginning to doubt the wisdom of capital punishment?"

Sullivan Stanley was not beginning to doubt anything of the kind. The reason for the peculiar expression on his face as he passed judgment on that autumn afternoon in 1947 was that, for the first time in some years, he had an erection as he spoke; he had an involuntary orgasm.

It was said that a man who was hanged automatically had an erection at the moment of the drop. Justice Stanley pondered this piece of information. He wondered if it was true. However that might be, he could find no connection with his own experience at passing sentence. But whenever, throughout the months and years to come, he thought about this case, he felt an inexplicable excitement.

The murderer, George Forrester, had stayed, as everyone knew, at the Rosemary Lawns Hotel in North London. It was there he had met the last of his victims, and the discovery of her body and the clues he furnished led to the other bodies. During the course of the trial, Justice Stanley had by way of a working scruple deliberately gone to look at the hotel from the outside. It was small, private, moderately priced, refined, and did not seem to deserve the two policemen who stood outside the entrance during the trial to keep the press and other intrusive elements from bothering those few remaining guests who had not packed up and fled as soon as the mud-river murder case hit the headlines.

In court, the manager gave evidence. A man of good presence, aged thirty-five, direct and frank, he impressed Justice Stanley in inverse proportion to the contempt the judge felt for George Forrester, the man at the bar. Justice Stanley usually despised the accused on some account or other quite distinct from the facts of the case. This time, it was the bright-brown, almost orange Harris tweed coat that the prisoner wore, in addition to his rusty-brown little moustache.

In 1947 George Forrester managed to murder three women in one year. Before that, he had no criminal record whatsoever. He was a commercial traveler in fishing tackle and gear, and apparently, according to his frightened and helpless wife, was in the habit of going off fishing in rivers throughout the country, wherever he happened to be at the end of a working week. His victims, three in all, were discovered shot in the head among reedy marshes where he had been seen wearing waders, plying his rod.

The three victims had in common that they were large, overweight women, widowed and middle-aged. George Forrester met them all in medium-priced genteel hotels where the guests had a fixed arrangement. His object was to rob the women of their jewelry and the contents of their handbags, and this he did in all three cases. The last case, that of Mrs. Emily Crathie, was the one for which he was tried before Justice Stanley. An interesting feature of the case was that George Forrester claimed to have had sex with Mrs. Crathie before bringing her to her muddy death among the reeds, although the forensic evidence argued against any sexual activity.

George Forrester admitted that he had offered Mrs. Crathie "a day out fishing." She occupied the next table to his at the Rosemary Lawns Hotel. This had been noticed by the manager and his wife and also by some of the other permanent clients. Her sudden absence was also noticed and, after a few days, reported to the police, no relatives being known.

In Mrs. Crathie's case the killer had been obliged to transport her body, minus her considerable diamond solitaire ring and other possessions, from his car to a part of a river in Norfolk where the reeds and banks were thicker than at the equally tranquil spot where he had killed her by pistol shot in the back of the head. The other two women had been killed and concealed in much the same way, but in the case of Mrs. Crathie it was a mystery, never to be explained by the investigative brains of England, how George Forrester, a slight man, had managed to convey massive Mrs. Crathie from her death place to his car and from his car to her grave among the reeds.

The hue and cry for the three missing women was afoot when George presented himself at a Norfolk police station with a mud-stained size-42 full bra, claiming he had fished it up when trying out his tackle on some water stretch of the county. The police interrogated George Forrester who, according to psychological explanations, had "wanted" to be caught and, in fact, thus *was* caught. The specimen of bra had been purchased by George himself from a nearby ladies' garments store, and, curiously, he had got Mrs. Crathie's measurement right.

Justice Stanley listened to all this, back in 1947, summed up, took the verdict, passed judgment—death by hanging—and experienced an inexplicable orgasm. He remembered it frequently from that day onwards.

Sir Sullivan Stanley (he had been knighted) was in his mid-fifties at the time of George Forrester's trial. The death penalty in England was afterwards abolished, and so there was no further call for Sir Sullivan to experience another such orgasm. Lady Stanley was some years older than her husband, just past her sixties. She was known everywhere as a good lady full of charitable activities such as prison visiting, the governing of schools, the organizing of soup kitchens. She had borne one son, now a lawyer in private practice. Sex in her life was a thing of the past; in fact, her recurring bouts of rheumatism prevented her from sharing anyone's bed.

At that time, Sir Sullivan frequented a lady who was known to the legal profession and who occasionally kept an afternoon for him. Lady Stanley suspected nothing of her existence, nor did she need to know. The affair, if it could be called that, between Sir Sullivan and Mary Spike, the lady in question, was something of an animated cartoon. She induced a mild sensation in the Justice; nothing more. Lady Stanley did not think for a moment that her husband could have another woman. She felt he was too pompous to take off his trousers in another person's house, and in this she was almost right.

After the death of Lady Stanley, Sir Sullivan, approaching his seventies, now visited Mary Spike occasionally, but just for the visit. The unusual circumstances of his sexual experience on the sentencing of George Forrester had really taken him by surprise.

He often thought back on the day when he had that orgasm in court. What happened to that gratuitous orgasm? Where was it now? It was like a butterfly fluttering away into the summer, always eluding the net. It even occurred to him that he might achieve one orgasm more before he died, by hanging himself. But it was problematic whether the phenomenon of an erection would amount to the sensation of an orgasm in a man whose neck was on the point of breaking, if not already broken. Besides, the secretly distraught judge mused, a suicide would look so bad in the *Times* obituary. Not to be thought of.

When Sir Sullivan retired he stayed for a while with his son in Hampstead. But this didn't work well. He decided to go and live in a residential hotel, and it was with great excitement that he discovered that the Rosemary Lawns Hotel was still functioning. Memories of the trial of

George Forrester came back to him ever more vividly.

The Rosemary Lawns Hotel sparkled with new paint the day the Judge went to seek a room there. The "Lawns" referred evidently to a tennis court, adjacent to the hotel, and an equal-sized stretch of flower-bordered lawn on the other side of a gravel path. It was early autumn, and the leaves scuttled along the tree-lined street. Some schoolgirls were chirpily playing tennis.

Sir Sullivan asked for the manager. A short figure came out of the back office. His white hair and slightly thickened appearance at first, and only for a moment, concealed the fact that this was probably the very man, the actual proprietor of the hotel, who had given evidence in court all those years ago.

"Are you Mr. Roger Cook?" inquired the Justice.

"Yes, indeed, sir."

"Good afternoon. I'm Sir Sullivan Stanley."

"The Judge! Sir Sullivan, you don't show your years."

"Yes, I'm the Judge himself. I have been here before, you know. At the time of the trial, when I came to case the joint, if I may use a vulgarism."

"Sir Sullivan," said Roger Cook, "it was a very hard time for us. All the permanent clients left. We thought of changing the name of the hotel, but we sat it out. We were especially grateful to you for that reference to Rosemary Lawns Hotel in your summing up."

"What was that?" said Sir Sullivan.

"You said we were a perfectly respectable place, clean and cosy. That it was no reflection on the establishment that the accused and his unfortunate victim happened to have taken up their abode at Rosemary Lawns. I recall the very words," said Roger Cook. "We always quoted them to the press when we gave interviews in those tragic weeks."

"Well, I congratulate you on the appearance of the place. I am glad to see the tennis court is being used."

"We rent out the court on certain days to a private school," said Roger Cook.

"Well, I'll be direct," said Sir Sullivan Stanley. "I'm looking for a comfortable place for my retirement. A fairly large room, bath and television. And, of course, a dining room. If you don't have the dining room any more, I'm afraid it's no good. To me, the dining room is essential."

"But of course, Sir Sullivan, we have the same dining room. Nothing's changed except the decoration. Come with me. It would be an honor to have you here."

He led the way to the dining room, where the tables were laid for dinner with pink cloths. On one table stood a bottle of Milk of Magnesia, but that alone was not enough evidence against the quality of the dinner. Roger Cook showed Sir Sullivan the menu: mulligatawny soup, followed by breast of lamb, peas and potatoes. Cheese (if required—extra charge according to choice), and strawberry or vanilla ice cream. Coffee or decaffeinated, as desired. Tea on request.

Sir Sullivan said, "Which of those tables did George Forrester occupy?"

"The third on the right under the window if I'm not mistaken. And poor Mrs. Crathie's was the next table to his, second on the right. Of course, we hold receptions, and so on. We use the supplementary dining room."

"The table by the window looks delightful," said Sir Sullivan with an air of decided nonchalance. "Nice outlook."

The proprietor, somewhat puzzled that the old Judge would actually prefer to sit in the murderer's chair, nevertheless made haste to assure the Judge that that particular table was not occupied by permanent *pensionnaires* at that moment.

So Sir Sullivan Stanley made an agreeable arrangement with the hotel and moved in the following Monday. He came down to dinner at quarter to eight to find the dining room three-quarters full and some of the diners already nearing the end of the meal.

A middle-aged woman with a long neck sat at the table next to his. She had reached the coffee stage.

"Good evening," said the Justice.

She responded with a kind of extra warmth, as if she approved of this gentleman, it being somewhat of a lottery who one got at the next table.

The waiter brought Sir Sullivan's soup.

The Justice turned to his neighbor, "Are you by any chance," he said, "Mrs. Crathie?"

"No, my name is Mrs. Morton. Do I resemble a friend of yours?"

"No—no friend. Just a person."

Sir Sullivan felt happy in her company. There was a small fire at the end of the dining room. Cosy. He thought of the schoolgirls who had been playing tennis outside, so encouraging to look at. He thought then of Mary Spike, his part-time mistress of so many years ago, and remembered how one afternoon when he had failed to come up to scratch she had cruelly laughed at him. "What an antique pendant you've got there. Talk about hanging judge! You're the hanging judge!"

Justice Stanley, seated at the late George Forrester's table, where the man had once sat wearing that bright-brown Harris tweed coat, looked at and partook of his mulligatawny soup. Then he looked across at Mrs. Morton with the greatest surprise—transfixed in a dreamy joy, as if he had seen a welcome ghost.

Mrs. Morton sipped her coffee and looked at him.

THE SERAPH AND
THE ZAMBESI

YOU MAY HAVE HEARD of Samuel
Cramer, half poet, half journalist, who had to
do with a dancer called the Fanfarlo. But, as you
will see, it doesn't matter if you have not. He was
said to be going strong in Paris early in the nine-
teenth century, and when I met him in 1946 he
was still going strong, but this time in a different
way. He was the same man, but modified. For in-
stance, in those days, more than a hundred years
ago, Cramer had persisted for several decades, and
without affectation, in being about twenty-five
years old. But when I knew him he was clearly undergoing his forty-two-year-old phase.

At this time he was keeping a gasoline pump
some four miles south of the Zambesi River where

it crashes over a precipice at the Victoria Falls. Cramer had some spare rooms where he put up visitors to the Falls when the hotel was full. I was sent to him because it was Christmas week and there was no room in the hotel.

I found him trying the starter of a large, lumpy Mercedes outside his corrugated-iron garage, and at first sight I judged him to be a Belgian from the Congo. He had the look of north and south, light hair with canvas-colored skin. Later, however, he told me that his father was German and his mother Chilean. It was this information rather than the "S. Cramer" above the garage door which made me think I had heard of him.

The rains had been very poor and that December was fiercely hot. On the third night before Christmas I sat on the porch outside my room, looking through the broken mosquito-wire network at the lightning in the distance. When an atmosphere maintains an excessive temperature for a long spell something seems to happen to the natural noises of life. Sound fails to carry in its usual quantity, but comes as if bound and gagged. That night the Christmas beetles, which fall on their backs on every porch with a high tic-tac, seemed to be shock-absorbed. I saw one fall and the little bump reached my ears a fraction behind time. The noises of minor wild beasts from the bush were all hushed-up, too. In fact it wasn't until the bush noises all stopped simultaneously, as they frequently do when a leopard is about, that I knew there had been any sound at all.

Overlying this general muted hum, Cramer's sundowner party progressed farther up the porch. The heat distorted every word. The glasses made a tinkle that was not of the substance of glass, but of bottles wrapped in tissue paper. Sometimes, for a moment, a shriek or a cackle would hang torpidly in space, but these were unreal sounds, as if projected from a distant country, as if they were pocket-torches seen through a London fog.

Cramer came over to my end of the porch and asked me to join his party. I said I would be glad to, and meant it, even though I had been glad to sit alone. Heat so persistent and so intense sucks up the will.

Five people sat in wicker armchairs drinking high-balls and chewing salted peanuts. I recognized a red-haired trooper from Livingstone, just out from England, and two of Cramer's lodgers, a tobacco planter and his wife from Bulawayo. In the custom of those parts, the other two were introduced by their first names. Mannie, a short dark man of square face and build, I thought might be a Portuguese from the east coast. The woman, Fanny, was picking bits out of the frayed wicker chair and as she lifted her glass her hand shook a little, making her bracelets chime. She would be about fifty, a well-tended woman, very neat. Her grey hair, tinted with blue, was done in a fringe above a face puckered with malaria.

In the general way of passing the time with strangers in that countryside, I exchanged with the tobacco people the names of acquaintances who lived within a six-hundred-mile radius of where we sat, reducing this list to names mutually known to us. The trooper contributed his news from the region between Lusaka and Livingstone. Meanwhile an argument was in process between Cramer, Fanny and Mannie, of which Fanny seemed to be getting the better. It appeared there was to be a play or concert on Christmas Eve in which the three were taking part. I several times heard the words "troupe of angels," "shepherds," "ridiculous price" and "my girls" which seemed to be key words in the argument. Suddenly, on hearing the trooper mention a name, Fanny broke off her talk and turned to us.

"She was one of my girls," she said, "I gave her lessons for three years."

Mannie rose to leave, and before Fanny followed him she picked a card from her handbag and held it out to me between her fingernails.

"If any of your friends are interested . . ." said Fanny hazily.

I looked at this as she drove off with the man, and above an address about four miles up the river I read:

> *Mme La Fanfarlo (Paris, London)*
> *Dancing Instructress. Ballet. Ballroom.*
> *Transport provided By Arrangement.*

Next day I came across Cramer still trying to locate the trouble with the Mercedes.

"Are you the man Baudelaire wrote about?" I asked him.

He stared past me at the open waste veldt with a look of tried patience.

"Yes," he replied. "What made you think of it?"

"The name Fanfarlo on Fanny's card," I said. "Didn't you know her in Paris?"

"Oh, yes," said Cramer, "but those days are finished. She married Manuela de Monteverde—that's Mannie. They settled here about twenty years ago. He keeps a Kaffir store."

I remembered then that in the Romantic age it had pleased Cramer to fluctuate between the practice of verse and that of belles lettres, together with the living up to such practices.

I asked him, "Have you given up your literary career?"

"*As* a career, yes," he answered. "It was an obsession I was glad to get rid of."

He stroked the blunt bonnet of the Mercedes and added, "The greatest literature is the occasional kind, a mere after-thought."

Again he looked across the veldt where, unseen, a grey-crested lourie was piping "go'way, go'way."

"Life," Cramer continued, "is the important thing."

"And do you write occasional verses?" I enquired.

"When occasion demands it," he said. "In fact I've just written a Nativity Masque. We're giving a performance on Christmas Eve in there." He pointed to his garage, where a few natives were already beginning to shift gasoline cans and tires. Being members neither of the cast nor the audience, they were taking their time. A pile of folded seats had been dumped alongside.

Late on the morning of Christmas Eve I returned from the Falls to find a crowd of natives quarrelling outside the garage, with Cramer swearing loud and heavy in the middle. He held a sulky man by the shirt-sleeve, while with the other hand he described his vituperation on the hot air.

Some mission natives had been sent over to give a hand with laying the stage, and these, with their standard-three school English, washed faces and white drill shorts, had innocently provoked Cramer's raw rag-dressed boys. Cramer's method, which ended with the word "police," succeeded in sending them back to work, still uttering drum-like gutturals at each other.

The stage, made of packing-cases with planks nailed across, was being put at the back of the building, where a door led to the yard, the privy and the native huts. The space between this door and the stage was closed off by a row of black Government blankets hung on a line; this was to be the dressing-room. I agreed to come round there that evening to help with the lighting, the make-up, and the pinning on of angels' wings. The Fanfarlo's dancing pupils were to make an angel chorus with carols and dancing, while she herself, as the Virgin, was to give a representative ballet performance. Owing to her husband's very broken English, he had been given a silent role as a shepherd, supported by three other shepherds chosen for like reasons. Cramer's part was the most prominent, for he had the longest speeches, being the First Seraph. It had been agreed that, since he had written the masque, he could best deliver most of it; but I gathered there had been some trouble at rehearsals over the cost of the production, with Fanny wanting elaborate scenery as being due to her girls.

The performance was set to begin at eight. I arrived behind the stage at seven-fifteen to find the angels assembled in ballet dresses with wings of crinkled paper in various shades. The Fanfarlo wore a long white transparent skirt with a sequin top. I was helping to fix on the Wise Men's beards when I saw Cramer. He had on a toga-like garment made up of several thicknesses of mosquito-net, but not thick enough to hide his white shorts underneath. He had put on his make-up early, and this was melting on his face in the rising heat.

"I always get nerves at this point," he said. "I'm going to practise my opening speech."

I heard him mount the stage and begin reciting. Above the voices of excited children I could only hear the rhythm of his voice; and I was intent on helping the Fanfarlo to paint her girls' faces. It seemed impossible. As fast as we lifted the sticks of paint they turned liquid. It was really getting abnormally hot.

"Open that door," yelled the Fanfarlo. The back door was opened and a crowd of curious natives pressed round the entrance. I left the Fanfarlo ordering them off, for I was determined to get to the front of the building for some air. I mounted the stage and began to cross it when I was aware of a powerful radiation of heat coming from my right. Looking round, I saw Cramer apparently shouting at someone, in the attitude of his dealings with the natives that morning. But he could not advance because of this current of heat. And because of the heat I could not at first make out who Cramer was rowing with; this was the sort of heat that goes for the eyes. But as I got further toward the front of the stage I saw what was standing there.

This was a living body. The most noticeable thing was its constancy; it seemed not to conform to the law of perspective, but remained the same size when I approached as when I withdrew. And altogether unlike other forms of life, it had a completed look. No part was undergoing a process; the outline lacked the signs of confusion and ferment which commonly indicate living things, and this was also the principle of its beauty. The eyes took up nearly the whole of the head, extending far over the cheekbones. From the back of the head came two muscular wings which from time to time folded themselves over the eyes, making a draught of scorching air. There was hardly any neck. Another pair of wings, tough and supple, spread from below the shoulders, and a third pair extended from the calves of the legs, appearing to sustain the body. The feet looked too fragile to bear up such a concentrated degree of being.

European residents of Africa are often irresistibly prompted to speak kitchen Kaffir to anything strange.

"Hamba!" shouted Cramer, meaning "Go away."

"Now get off the stage and stop your noise," said the living body peaceably.

"Who in hell are you?" said Cramer, gasping through the heat.

"The same as in Heaven," came the reply, "a Seraph, that's to say."

"Tell that to someone else," Cramer panted. "Do I look like a fool?"

"I will. No, nor a Seraph either," said the Seraph.

The place was filling with heat from the Seraph. Cramer's paint was running into his eyes and he wiped them on his net robe. Walking backward to a less hot place he cried, "Once and for all—"

"That's correct," said the Seraph.

"—this is my show," continued Cramer.

"Since when?" the Seraph said.

"Right from the start," Cramer breathed at him.

"Well, it's been mine from the Beginning," said the Seraph, "and the Beginning began first."

Climbing down from the hot stage, Cramer caught his seraphic robe on a nail and tore it. "Listen here," he said, "I can't conceive of an abnormality like you being a true Seraph."

"True," said the Seraph.

By this time I had been driven by the heat to the front entrance. Cramer joined me there. A number of natives had assembled. The audience had begun to arrive in cars and the rest of the cast had come round the building from the back. It was impossible to see far inside the building owing to the Seraph's heat, and impossible to re-enter.

Cramer was still haranguing the Seraph from the door, and there was much speculation among the new arrivals as to which of the three familiar categories the present trouble came under, namely, the natives, Whitehall, or leopards.

"This is my property," cried Cramer, "and these people have paid for their seats. They've come to see a masque."

"In that case," said the Seraph, "I'll cool down and they can come and see a masque."

"*My* masque," said Cramer.

"Ah, no, *mine*," said the Seraph. "Yours won't do."

"Will you go, or shall I call the police?" said Cramer with finality.

"I have no alternative," said the Seraph more finally still.

Word had gone round that a mad leopard was in the garage. People got back into their cars and parked at a safe distance; the tobacco planter went to fetch a gun. A number of young troopers had the idea of blinding the mad leopard with gasoline and ganged up some natives to fill gasoline cans from the pump and pass them chainwise to the garage.

"This'll fix him," said a trooper.

"That's right, let him have it," said Cramer from his place by the door.

"I shouldn't do that," said the Seraph. "You'll cause a fire."

The first lot of gasoline to be flung into the heat flared up. The seats caught alight first, then the air itself began to burn within the metal walls till the whole interior was flame feeding on flame. Another carload of troopers arrived just then and promptly got a gang of natives to fill gasoline cans with water. Slowly they drenched the fire. The Fanfarlo mustered her angels a little way up the road. She was trying to reassure their parents and see what was happening at the same time, furious at losing her opportunity to dance. She aimed a hard poke at the back of one of the angels whose parents were in England.

It was some hours before the fire was put out. While the corrugated metal walls still glowed, twisted and furled, it was impossible to see what had happened to the Seraph, and after they had ceased to glow it was too dark and hot to see far into the wreck.

"Are you insured?" one of Cramer's friends asked him.

"Oh yes," Cramer replied, "my policy covers everything except Acts of God—that means lightning or flood."

"He's fully covered," said Cramer's friend to another friend.

Many people had gone home and the rest were going. The troopers drove off singing "Good King Wenceslaus," and the mission boys ran down the road singing "Good Christian Men, Rejoice."

It was about midnight, and still very hot. The tobacco planters suggested a drive to the Falls, where it was cool. Cramer and the Fanfarlo joined us, and we bumped along the rough path from Cramer's to the main highway. There the road is tarred only in two strips to take car-wheels. The thunder of the Falls reached us about two miles before we reached them.

"After all my work on the masque and everything!" Cramer was saying.

"Oh, shut up," said the Fanfarlo.

Just then, by the glare of our headlights I saw the Seraph again, going at about seventy miles an hour and skimming the tarmac strips with two of his six wings in swift motion, two folded over his face, and two covering his feet.

"That's him!" said Cramer. "We'll get him yet."

We left the car near the hotel and followed a track through the dense vegetation of the Rain Forest, where the spray from the Falls descends perpetually. It was like a convalescence after fever, that frail rain after the heat. The Seraph was far ahead of us and through the trees I could see where his heat was making steam of the spray.

We came to the cliff's edge, where opposite us and from the same level the full weight of the river came blasting into the gorge between. There was no sign of the Seraph. Was he far below in the heaving pit, or where?

Then I noticed that along the whole mile of the waterfall's crest the spray was rising higher than usual. This I took to be steam from the Seraph's heat. I was right, for presently, by the mute flashes of summer lightning we watched him ride the Zambesi away from us, among the rocks that look like crocodiles and the crocodiles that look like rocks.

THE LEAF-SWEEPER

BEHIND THE TOWN HALL there is a wooded parkland which, toward the end of November, begins to draw a thin blue cloud right into itself; and as a rule the park floats in this haze until mid-February. I pass every day, and see Johnnie Geddes in the heart of this mist, sweeping up the leaves. Now and again he stops, and jerking his long head erect, looks indignantly at the pile of leaves, as if it ought not to be there; then he sweeps on. This business of leaf-sweeping he learned during the years he spent in the asylum; it was the job they always gave him to do; and when he was discharged the town council gave him the leaves to sweep. But the indignant movement of the head comes naturally to him, for this has been one of his habits since he was the most promising and buoyant and vociferous graduate of his year. He looks much older than he is, for it is not quite twenty years ago that Johnnie founded the Society for the Abolition of Christmas.

Johnnie was living with his aunt then. I was at school, and in the Christmas holidays Miss Geddes gave me her nephew's pamphlet, *How to Grow Rich at Christmas*. It sounded very likely, but it turned out that you grow rich at Christmas by doing away with Christmas, and so pondered Johnnie's pamphlet no further.

But it was only his first attempt. He had, within the next three years, founded his society of Abolitionists. His new book, *Abolish Christmas or We Die*, was in great demand at the public library, and my turn for it came at last. Johnnie was really convincing, this time, and most people were completely won over until after they had closed the book. I got an old copy for sixpence the other day, and despite the lapse of time it still proves conclusively that Christmas is a national crime. Johnnie demonstrates that every human-unit in the kingdom faces inevitable starvation within a period inversely proportional to that in which one in every six industrial-productivity units, if you see what he means, stops producing toys to fill the stockings of the educational-intake units. He cites appalling statistics to show that 1.024 per cent of the time squandered each Christmas in reckless shopping and thoughtless churchgoing brings the nation closer to its doom by five years. A few readers protested, but Johnnie was able to demolish their muddled arguments, and meanwhile the Society for the Abolition of Christmas increased. But Johnnie was troubled. Not only did Christmas rage throughout the kingdom as usual that year, but he had private information that many of the Society's members had broken the Oath of Abstention.

He decided, then, to strike at the very roots of Christmas. Johnnie gave up his job on the Drainage Supply Board; he gave up all his prospects, and, financed by a few supporters, retreated for two years to study the roots of Christmas. Then, all jubilant, Johnnie produced his next and last book, in which he established, either that Christmas was an invention of the Early Fathers to propitiate the pagans, or it was invented by the pagans to placate the Early Fathers, I forget which. Against the advice of his friends, Johnnie entitled it *Christmas and Christianity*. It sold eighteen copies. Johnnie never really recovered from this; and it happened, about that time, that the girl he was engaged to, an ardent Abolitionist, sent him a pullover she had knitted, for Christmas; he sent it back, enclosing a copy of the Society's rules, and she sent back the ring. But in any case, during Johnnie's absence, the Society had been undermined by a moderate faction. These moderates finally became more moderate, and the whole thing broke up.

Soon after this, I left the district, and it was some years before I saw Johnnie again. One Sunday afternoon in summer, I was idling among the crowds who were gathered to hear the speakers at Hyde Park. One little crowd surrounded a man who bore a banner marked "Crusade against Christmas"; his voice was frightening; it carried an unusually long way. This was Johnnie. A man in the crowd told me Johnnie was there every Sunday, very violent about Christmas, and that he would soon be taken up for insulting language. As I saw in the papers, he was soon taken up for insulting language. And a few months later I heard that poor Johnnie was in a mental home, because he had Christmas on the brain and couldn't stop shouting about it.

After that I forgot all about him until three years ago, in December, I went to live near the town where Johnnie had spent his youth. On the afternoon of Christmas Eve I was walking with a friend, noticing what had changed in my absence, and what hadn't. We passed a long, large house, once famous for its armoury, and I saw that the iron gates were wide open.

"They used to be kept shut," I said.

"That's an asylum now," said my friend; "they let the mild cases work in the grounds, and leave the gates open to give them a feeling of freedom."

"But," said my friend, "they lock everything inside. Door after door. The lift as well; they keep it locked."

While my friend was chattering, I stood in the gateway and looked in. Just beyond the gate was a great bare elm-tree. There I saw a man in brown corduroys, sweeping up the leaves. Poor soul, he was shouting about Christmas.

"That's Johnnie Geddes," I said. "Has he been here all these years?"

"Yes," said my friend as we walked on. "I believe he gets worse at this time of year."

"Does his aunt see him?"

"Yes. And she sees nobody else."

We were, in fact, approaching the house where Miss Geddes lived. I suggested we call on her. I had known her well.

"No fear," said my friend.

I decided to go in, all the same, and my friend walked on to the town.

Miss Geddes had changed, more than the landscape. She had been a solemn, calm woman, and now she moved about quickly, and gave short agitated smiles. She took me to her sitting-room, and as she opened the door she called to someone inside,

"Johnnie, see who's come to see us!"

A man, dressed in a dark suit, was standing on a chair, fixing holly behind a picture. He jumped down.

"Happy Christmas," he said. "A Happy and a Merry Christmas indeed. I do hope," he said, "you're going to stay for tea, as we've got a delightful Christmas cake, and at this season of goodwill I would be cheered indeed if you could see how charmingly it's decorated; it has "Happy Christmas" in red icing, and then there's a robin and—"

"Johnnie," said Miss Geddes, "you're forgetting the carols."

"The carols," he said. He lifted a gramophone record from a pile and put it on. It was "The Holly and the Ivy."

"It's 'The Holly and the Ivy,'" said Miss Geddes. "Can't we have something else? We had that all morning."

"It is sublime," he said, beaming from his chair, and holding up his hand for silence.

While Miss Geddes went to fetch the tea, and he sat absorbed in his carol, I watched him. He was so like Johnnie, that if I hadn't seen poor Johnnie a few moments before, sweeping up the asylum leaves, I would have thought he really was Johnnie. Miss Geddes returned with the tray, and while he rose to put on another record, he said something that startled me.

"I saw you in the crowd that Sunday when I was speaking at Hyde Park."

"What a memory you have!" said Miss Geddes.

"It must be ten years ago," he said.

"My nephew has altered his opinion of Christmas," she explained. "He always comes home for Christmas now, and don't we have a jolly time, Johnnie?"

"Rather!" he said. "Oh, let me cut the cake."

He was very excited about the cake. With a flourish he dug a large knife into the side. The knife slipped, and I saw it run deep into his finger. Miss Geddes did not move. He wrenched his cut finger away, and went on slicing the cake.

"Isn't it bleeding?" I said.

He held up his hand. I could see the deep cut, but there was no blood.

Deliberately, and perhaps desperately, I turned to Miss Geddes.

"That house up the road," I said, "I see it's a mental home now. I passed it this afternoon."

"Johnnie," said Miss Geddes, as one who knows the game is up, "go and fetch the mince-pies."

He went, whistling a carol.

"You passed the asylum," said Miss Geddes wearily.

"Yes," I said.

"And you saw Johnnie sweeping up the leaves."

"Yes."

We could still hear the whistling of the carol.

"Who is *he*?" I said.

"That's Johnnie's ghost," she said. "He comes home every Christmas. But," she said, "I don't like him. I can't bear him any longer, and I'm going away tomorrow. I don't want Johnnie's ghost, I want Johnnie in flesh and blood."

I shuddered, thinking of the cut finger that could not bleed. And I left, before Johnnie's ghost returned with the mince-pies.

Next day, as I had arranged to join a family who lived in the town, I started walking over about noon. Because of the light mist, I didn't see at first who it was approaching. It was a man, waving his arm to me. It turned out to be Johnnie's ghost.

"Happy Christmas. What do you think," said Johnnie's ghost, "my aunt has gone to London. Fancy, on Christmas day, and I thought she was at church, and here I am without anyone to spend a jolly Christmas with, and, of course, I forgive her, as it's the season of goodwill, but I'm glad to see you, because now I can come with you, wherever it is you're going, and we can all have a Happy . . ."

"Go away," I said, and walked on.

It sounds hard. But perhaps you don't know how repulsive and loathsome is the ghost of a living man. The ghosts of the dead may be all right, but the ghost of mad Johnnie gave me the creeps.

"Clear off," I said.

He continued walking beside me. "As it's the time of goodwill, I make allowances for your tone," he said. "But I'm coming."

We had reached the asylum gates, and there, in the grounds, I saw Johnnie sweeping the leaves. I suppose it was his way of going on strike, working on Christmas day. He was making a noise about Christmas.

On a sudden impulse I said to Johnnie's ghost, "You want company?"

"Certainly," he replied. "It's the season of . . ."

"Then you shall have it," I said.

I stood in the gateway. "Oh, Johnnie," I called. He looked up.

"I've brought your ghost to see you, Johnnie."

"Well, well," said Johnnie, advancing to meet his ghost. "Just imagine it!"

"Happy Christmas," said Johnnie's ghost.

"Oh, really?" said Johnnie.

I left them to it. And when I looked back, wondering if they would come to blows, I saw that Johnnie's ghost was sweeping the leaves as well. They seemed to be arguing at the same time. But it was still misty, and really, I can't say whether, when I looked a second time, there were two men or one man sweeping the leaves.

Johnnie began to improve in the New Year. At least, he stopped shouting about Christmas, and then he never mentioned it at all; in a few months, when he had almost stopped saying anything, they discharged him.

The town council gave him the leaves of the park to sweep. He seldom speaks, and recognizes nobody. I see him every day at the late end of the year, working within the mist. Sometimes, if there is a sudden gust, he jerks his head up to watch a few leaves falling behind him, as if amazed that they are undeniably there, although, by rights, the falling of leaves should be stopped.

THE HOUSE OF
THE FAMOUS POET

IN THE SUMMER OF 1944, when it was
nothing for trains from the provinces to be five
or six hours late, I traveled to London on the night
train from Edinburgh, which, at York, was already
three hours late. There were ten people in the com-
partment, only two of whom I remember well, and
for good reason.

I have the impression, looking back on it, of a
row of people opposite me, dozing untidily with
heads askew, and, as it often seems when we look
at sleeping strangers, their features had assumed
extra emphasis and individuality, sometimes dis-
turbing to watch. It was as if they had rendered up
their daytime talent for obliterating the outward
traces of themselves in exchange for mental oblit-

eration. In this way they resembled a twelfth-century fresco; there was a look of medieval un-selfconsciousness about these people, all except one.

This was a private soldier who was awake to a greater degree than most people are when they are not sleeping. He was smoking cigarettes one after the other with long, calm puffs. I thought he looked excessively evil—an atavistic type. His forehead must have been less than two inches high above dark, thick eyebrows, which met. His jaw was not large, but it was apelike; so was his small nose and so were his deep, close-set eyes. I thought there must have been some consanguinity in the parents. He was quite a throwback.

As it turned out, he was extremely gentle and kind. When I ran out of cigarettes, he fished about in his haversack and produced a packet for me and one for a girl sitting next to me. We both tried, with a flutter of small change, to pay him. Nothing would please him at all but that we should accept his cigarettes, whereupon he returned to his silent, reflective smoking.

I felt a sort of pity for him then, rather as we feel toward animals we know to be harmless, such as monkeys. But I realized that, like the pity we expend on monkeys merely because they are not human beings, this pity was not needed.

Receiving the cigarettes gave the girl and myself common ground, and we conversed quietly for the rest of the journey. She told me she had a job in London as a domestic helper and nursemaid. She looked as if she had come from a country district—her very blonde hair, red face and large bones gave the impression of power, as if she was used to carrying heavy things, perhaps great scuttles of coal, or two children at a time. But what made me curious about her was her voice, which was cultivated, melodious and restrained.

Toward the end of the journey, when the people were beginning to jerk themselves straight and the rushing to and fro in the corridor had started, this girl, Elise, asked me to come with her to the house where she worked. The master, who was something in a university, was away with his wife and family.

I agreed to this, because at that time I was in the way of thinking that the discovery of an educated servant girl was valuable and something to be gone deeper into. It had the element of experience—perhaps, even of truth—and I believed, in those days, that truth is stranger than fiction. Besides, I wanted to spend that Sunday in London. I was due back next day at my job in a branch of the civil service, which had been evacuated to the country and for a reason that is another story, I didn't want to return too soon. I had some telephoning to do. I wanted to wash and change. I wanted to know more about the girl. So I thanked Elise and accepted her invitation.

I regretted it as soon as we got out of the train at King's Cross, some minutes after ten. Standing up tall on the platform, Elise looked unbearably tired, as if not only the last night's journey but every fragment of her unknown life was suddenly heaping up on top of her. The power I had noticed in the train was no longer there. As she called, in her beautiful voice, for a porter, I saw that on the side of her head that had been away from me in the train, her hair was parted in a dark streak, which, by contrast with the yellow, looked navy blue. I had thought, when I first saw her, that possibly her hair was bleached, but now, seeing it so badly done, seeing this navy blue parting pointing like an arrow to the weighted weariness of her face, I, too, got the sensation of great tiredness. And it was not only the strain of the journey that I felt, but the foreknowledge of boredom that comes upon us unaccountably at the beginning of a quest, and that checks, perhaps mercifully, our curiosity.

And, as it happened, there really wasn't much to learn about Elise. The explanation of her that I had been prompted to seek, I got in the taxi between King's Cross and the house at Swiss Cottage. She came of a good family, who thought her a pity, and she them. Having no training for anything else, she had taken a domestic job on leaving home. She was engaged to an Australian soldier billeted also at Swiss Cottage.

Perhaps it was the anticipation of a day's boredom, maybe it was the effect of no sleep or the fact that the V-1 sirens were sounding, but I felt some sourness when I saw the house. The garden was growing all over the place. Elise opened the front door, and we entered a darkish room almost wholly taken up with a long, plain wooden worktable. On this were a half-empty marmalade jar, a pile of papers, and a dried-up ink bottle. There was a steel-canopied bed, known as a Morrison shelter, in one corner and some photographs on the mantelpiece, one of a schoolboy wearing glasses. Everything was tainted with Elise's weariness and my own distaste. But Elise didn't seem to be aware of the exhaustion so plainly revealed on her face. She did not even bother to take her coat off, and as it was too tight for her I wondered how she could move about so quickly with this restriction added to the weight of her tiredness. But, with her coat still buttoned tight Elise phoned her boyfriend and made breakfast, while I washed in a dim, blue, cracked bathroom upstairs.

When I found that she had opened my hold-all without asking me and had taken out my rations, I was a little pleased. It seemed a friendly action, with some measure of reality about it, and I felt better. But I was still irritated by the house. I felt there was no justification for the positive lack of consequence which was lying about here and there. I asked no question about the owner who was something in a university, for fear of getting the answer I expected—that he was away visiting his grandchildren, at some family gathering in the home counties. The owners of the house had no reality for me, and I looked upon the place as be-longing to, and permeated with, Elise.

I went with her to a nearby public house, where she met her boyfriend and one or two other Australian soldiers. They had with them a thin Cockney girl with bad teeth. Elise was very happy, and insisted in her lovely voice that they should all come along to a party at the house that evening. In a fine aristocratic tone, she demanded that each should bring a bottle of beer.

During the afternoon Elise said she was going to have a bath, and she showed me a room where I could use the telephone and sleep if I wanted. This was a large, light room with several windows, much more orderly than the rest of the house, and lined with books. There was only one unusual thing about it: beside one of the windows was a bed, but this bed was only a fairly thick mattress made up neatly on the floor. It was obviously a bed on the floor with some purpose, and again I was angered to think of the futile crankiness of the elderly professor who had thought of it.

I did my telephoning, and decided to rest. But first I wanted to find something to read. The books puzzled me. None of them seemed to be automatically part of a scholar's library. An inscription in one book was signed by the author, a well-known novelist. I found another inscribed copy, and this had the name of the recipient. On a sudden idea, I went to the desk, where while I had been telephoning I had noticed a pile of unopened letters. For the first time, I looked at the name of the owner of the house.

I ran to the bathroom and shouted through the door to Elise, "Is this the house of the famous poet?"

"Yes," she called. "I *told* you."

She had told me nothing of the kind. I felt I had no right at all to be there, for it wasn't, now, the house of Elise acting by proxy for some unknown couple. It was the house of a famous modern poet. The thought that at any moment he and his family might walk in and find me there terrified me. I insisted that Elise should open the bathroom

door and tell me to my face that there was no possible chance of their returning for many days to
come.

Then I began to think about the house itself,
which Elise was no longer accountable for. Its new
definition, as the house of a poet whose work I
knew well, many of whose poems I knew by heart,
gave it altogether a new appearance.

To confirm this, I went outside and stood exactly where I had been when I first saw the garden
from the door of the taxi. I wanted to get my first
impression for a second time.

And this time I saw an absolute purpose in the
overgrown garden, which, since then, I have come
to believe existed in the eye of the beholder. But, at
the time, the room we had first entered, and which
had riled me, now began to give back a meaning,
and whatever was, was right. The caked-up bottle
of ink, which Elise had put on the mantelpiece, I
replaced on the table to make sure. I saw a photograph I hadn't noticed before, and I recognized the
famous poet.

It was the same with the upstairs room where
Elise had put me, and I handled the books again,
not so much with the sense that they belonged to
the famous poet but with some curiosity about
how they had been made. The sort of question
that occurred to me was where the paper had

come from and from what sort of vegetation was manufactured the black print, and these things have not troubled me since.

The Australians and the Cockney girl came around about seven. I had planned to catch an eight-thirty train to the country, but when I telephoned to confirm the time I found there were no Sunday trains running. Elise, in her friendly and exhausted way, begged me to stay without attempting to be too serious about it. The sirens were starting up again. I asked Elise once more to repeat that the poet and his family could by no means return that night. But I asked this question more abstractedly than before, as I was thinking of the sirens and of the exact proportions of the noise they made. I wondered, as well, what sinister genius of the Home Office could have invented so ominous a wail, and why. And I was thinking of the word "siren." The sound then became comical, for I imagined some maniac sea nymph from centuries past belching into the year 1944. Actually, the sirens frightened me.

Most of all, I wondered about Elise's party. Everyone roamed about the place as if it were nobody's house in particular, with Elise the best-behaved of the lot. The Cockney girl sat on the long table and gave of her best to the skies every time a bomb exploded. I had the feeling that the house had been requisitioned for an evening by the military. It was so hugely and everywhere occupied that it became not the house I had first entered, nor the house of the famous poet, but a third house—the one I had vaguely prefigured when I stood, bored, on the platform at King's Cross Station. I saw a great amount of tiredness among these people, and heard, from the loud noise they made, that they were all lacking sleep. When the beer was finished and they were gone, some to their billets, some to pubs, and the Cockney girl to her Underground shelter where she had slept for weeks past, I asked Elise, "Don't you feel tired?"

"No," she said with agonizing weariness, "I never feel tired."

I fell asleep myself, as soon as I had got into the bed on the floor in the upstairs room, and overslept until Elise woke me at eight. I had wanted to get up early to catch a nine o'clock train, so I hadn't much time to speak to her. I did notice, though, that she had lost some of her tired look.

I was pushing my things into my hold-all while Elise went up the street to catch a taxi when I heard someone coming upstairs. I thought it was Elise come back, and I looked out of the open door. I saw a man in uniform carrying an enormous parcel in both hands. He looked down as he climbed, and had a cigarette in his mouth.

"Do you want Elise?" I called, thinking it was one of her friends.

He looked up, and I recognized the soldier, the throwback, who had given us cigarettes in the train.

"Well, anyone will do," he said. "The thing is, I've got to get back to camp and I'm stuck for the fare—eight and six."

I told him I could manage it, and was finding the money when he said, putting his parcel on the floor, "I don't want to borrow it. I wouldn't think of borrowing it. I've got something for sale."

"What's that?" I said.

"A funeral," said the soldier. "I've got it here."

This alarmed me, and I went to the window. No hearse, no coffin stood below. I saw only the avenue of trees.

The soldier smiled. "It's an abstract funeral," he explained, opening the parcel.

He took it out and I examined it carefully, greatly comforted. It was very much the sort of thing I had wanted—rather more purple in parts than I would have liked, for I was not in favor of this color of mourning. Still, I thought I could tone it down a bit.

Delighted with the bargain, I handed over the eight shillings and sixpence. There was a great deal of this abstract funeral. Hastily, I packed some of it into the hold-all. Some I stuffed in my pockets, and there was still some left over. Elise had returned with a cab and I hadn't much time. So I ran for it, out of the door and out of the gate of the house of the famous poet, with the rest of my funeral trailing behind me.

You will complain that I am withholding evidence. Indeed, you may wonder if there is any evidence at all. "An abstract funeral," you will say, "is neither here nor there. It is only a notion. You cannot pack a notion into your bag. You cannot see the color of a notion."

You will insinuate that what I have just told you is pure fiction.

Hear me to the end.

I caught the train. Imagine my surprise when I found, sitting opposite me, my friend the soldier, of whose existence you are so sceptical.

"As a matter of interest," I said, "how would you describe all this funeral you sold me?"

"Describe it?" he said. "Nobody describes an abstract funeral. You just conceive it."

"There is much in what you say," I replied. "Still, describe it I must, because it is not every day one comes by an abstract funeral."

"I am glad you appreciate that," said the soldier.

"And after the war," I continued, "when I am no longer a civil servant, I hope in a few deftly turned phrases, to write of my experiences at the house of the famous poet, which has culminated like this. But of course," I added, "I will need to say what it looks like."

The soldier did not reply.

"If it were an okapi or a sea-cow," I said, "I would have to say what it looked like. No one would believe me otherwise."

"Do you want your money back?" asked the soldier. "Because if so, you can't have it. I spent it on my ticket."

"Don't misunderstand me," I hastened to say. "The funeral is a delightful abstraction. Only, I wish to put it down in writing."

I felt a great pity for the soldier on seeing his worried look. The ape-like head seemed the saddest thing in the world.

"I make them by hand," he said, "these abstract funerals."

A siren sounded somewhere, far away.

"Elise bought one of them last month. She hadn't any complaints. I change at the next stop," he said, getting down his kit from the rack. "And what's more," he said, "your famous poet bought one."

"Oh, did he?" I said.

"Yes," he said. "No complaints. It was just what he wanted—the idea of a funeral."

The train pulled up. The soldier leaped down and waved. As the train started again, I unpacked my abstract funeral and looked at it for a few moments.

"To hell with the idea," I said. "It's a real funeral I want."

"All in good time," said a voice from the corridor.

"*You* again," I said. It was the soldier.

"No," he said, "I got off at the last station. I'm only a notion of myself."

"Look here," I said, "would you be offended if I throw all this away?"

"Of course not," said the soldier. "You can't offend a notion."

"I want a real funeral," I explained. "One of my own."

"That's right," said the soldier.

"And then I'll be able to write about it and go into all the details," I said.

"Your own funeral?" he said. "You want to write it up?"

"Yes," I said.

"But," said he, "you're only human. Nobody reports on their own funeral. It's got to be abstract."

"You see my predicament?" I said.

"I see it," he replied. "I get off at this stop."

This notion of a soldier alighted. Once more the train put on speed. Out of the window I chucked all my eight and sixpence worth of abstract funeral. I watched it fluttering over the fields and around the tops of camouflaged factories with the sun glittering richly upon it, until it was out of sight.

In the summer of 1944 a great many people were harshly and suddenly killed. The papers reported, in due course, those whose names were known to the public. One of these, the famous poet, had returned unexpectedly to his home at Swiss Cottage a few moments before it was hit direct by a flying bomb. Fortunately, he had left his wife and children in the country.

When I got to the place where my job was, I had some time to spare before going on duty. I decided to ring Elise and thank her properly, as I had left in such a hurry. But the lines were out of order, and the operator could not find words enough to express her annoyance with me. Behind this overworked quarrelsome voice from the exchange I heard the high, long hoot which means that the telephone at the other end is not functioning, and the sound made me infinitely depressed and weary; it was more intolerable to me than the sirens, and I replaced the receiver; and, in fact, Elise had already perished under the house of the famous poet.

The blue cracked bathroom, the bed on the floor, the caked ink bottle, the neglected garden, and the neat rows of books—I try to gather them together in my mind whenever I am enraged by the thought that Elise and the poet were killed outright. The angels of the Resurrection will invoke the dead man and the dead woman, but who will care to restore the fallen house of the famous poet if not myself? Who else will tell its story?

When I reflect how Elise and the poet were taken in—how they calmly allowed a well-meaning soldier to sell them the notion of a funeral, I remind myself that one day I will accept, and so will you, an abstract funeral, and make no complaints.

ANOTHER PAIR OF HANDS

I AM THE ONLY SON OF parents old enough to be grandparents. This has advantages and disadvantages, for although I was out of touch with the intervening generation, my mother's friends when I was born being forty and upwards and my father's contemporaries mostly over sixty, I inherited a longer sense of living history than most people do. It was quite natural for my elders to talk about the life of the early part of the century to which they belonged, and I grew up knowing instinctively how things were done in those days and how they thought.

My mother died aged ninety-six, just after my fiftieth birthday. She had survived my father by nearly thirty years. She was active almost to the last, the only difficulty being her failing eyesight; her movements had slowed down a bit. But really she was, as everyone said, wonderful for her age. She died quickly of a stroke. To the last she was still wondering why I hadn't found the right woman to marry. Maybe she's wondering even yet. She belonged to the wondering generation.

My mother, originally mistress of a great house with countless servants, had moved down with the times like everyone else, each move to a smaller house and fewer servants being somewhat of a trauma to her. She called every new house poky, every domestic arrangement makeshift. It was not till well after the First World War that she got used to only four indoor servants including a manservant and three outdoor. Somewhere about the end of the fifties she was reduced to a compact Georgian house in Sussex with twelve bedrooms surrounded by woodland. It became more and more enormous for one person as time went on. Her means were sufficient but she couldn't get the staff she needed. A few rooms were closed off entirely. Some years before she died she was doing very well with a gardener to keep going a token piece of lawn and some kitchen-garden patches, and, indoors, her cook-housekeeper, Miss Spigot, and Winnie the maid. By the end of her life, two years ago, she was left with only Winnie.

After Miss Spigot's death Winnie struggled on, in deep chaos, burning the food and quite unable to shop and clean. My mother wouldn't lift a finger beyond picking flowers; she sat calmly with her eternal sewing, which she called "my work," giving orders. Up to then I had been accustomed to go down to spend Sunday and Monday with a few friends to cheer Ma up, and she had always looked forward to these visits. She had outlived her sisters and her friends, and she enjoyed company. My own work, a regular theater column, prevented me from spending much more time with her. I don't notice dust but I do notice bad food; I must say Miss Spigot, who was already in her late seventies, had cooked very well. Our rooms had always been ready and bright when we arrived during Miss Spigot's lifetime. But suddenly all that ended. Winnie was frantic. I could see that my mother would have to move again. I begged her to let me get her a small flat in London. She was very old but by no means infirm, especially of purpose. "Winnie can manage alone. I shall have a Word with her," said Ma, and went on with her needlepoint or whatever. I could have killed her, but Ma wasn't the sort of person you could easily be nasty to.

I decided to stop bringing my friends to my mother's. My own visits were hell. There was a terrible smell everywhere of burnt food, unaired rooms and sheer neglect. My mother's tastes in food were simple and I dare say so were Winnie's, but as for me I like my square meals. The dining-room floor was littered with old bits of toast and egg-shells. The table hadn't been cleared for weeks, the place-mats were greasy. I did my best to help clear up on my miserable Sundays and Mondays. Personally, I'm quite used to shifting for myself in London; in fact, having been brought up with servants, I hate them. Your life's never your own. In London I always managed with a morning woman.

But I wasn't up to coping with a vast house like Ma's. Nothing would disturb Ma's resolve to put up with it or Winnie's exasperating loyalty; she took my mother's part. It went on for a month. I spent all my spare time in employment agencies and on various other means to get someone to replace Miss Spigot, but nothing came of my efforts or those of my friends; nothing. "I am going to have a Word with Winnie," said Ma.

On the fifth Sunday I drove down to Sussex late intending to cut short the horror of it all. Amazingly, there was no horror. Winnie had become a super-efficient cook-housekeeper all in the course of a week. As I passed the dining-room I could see the table was laid ready, sparkling with silver and glass, and the table-linen was up to Ma's best standard. The drawing-room was fresh and the windows looked like glass once more.

Ma was knitting. It was almost time to go in to dinner.

"Have you found someone to help?" I said.

"No," said Ma.

"Well, how has Winnie managed all this on her own?"

"I had a Word with her," said my mother.

Winnie served an excellent dinner on the whole; perhaps it wasn't quite up to the late cook's quality but certainly ambitious enough to include a rather flat soufflé.

"It's her first soufflé," said Ma, when Winnie went to get the meat course. "If she doesn't improve I'll have a Word."

But now something had happened to Winnie. She was perfectly happy, indeed almost blissful. She went around whispering to herself in a decidedly odd way. She served the vegetables with great care, but whispering, whispering, all the time.

"What did you say, Winnie?" I said.

"The soufflé was flat," said Winnie.

"Turn on the BBC news," said my mother.

For the whole of Monday Winnie went round chattering to herself. Breakfast was, however, set out on the table with nothing forgotten. The house was already in good order before half-past eight, the fire new and crackling. And Winnie conversed with herself, merrily, and quite a lot. I supposed that finding herself alone in the kitchen was now showing. However, my mother seemed to have solved her domestic problem which had fast been developing into mine. I didn't give time to worrying lest Winnie was turning a little funny.

I went back cheerfully to my own bachelor life and regaled my friends with the news of the change that had come over Winnie and of how well she was coping. They were quite eager to come and join me in Sussex again, assuring me they would make their own beds, help with the shopping and generally refrain from giving Winnie a hard time. I thought I'd better wait a few weeks before making up a party as of old. These visitors to my mother's house were either unmarried and younger colleagues of mine who, like myself, had to work on Saturdays for their newspapers, or middle-aged widows who had nothing to tie them to any day of the week. All were very keen to come, but I waited.

Winnie was even more efficient the next week. I came to the conclusion that it was Winnie who had been the guiding spirit in the kitchen all along; she was a good cook. Ma took no notice of her whatsoever, as was always her way, preferring not to praise or blame, just to give orders. Winnie was an unguessable age between fifty-five and seventy, her face was big with a lot of folds, her body thin and angular, her hair chocolate-rinsed. My mother who long ago had been used to picking and choosing maids "of good appearance" had taken some time to resign herself to uncomely Winnie, and, having done so, she was not now inclined to waste consideration on any further divergence from the norm that Winnie might display.

Winnie in fact could now be heard in the kitchen kicking up a dreadful racket. One evening the noise filled the house for about ten minutes. My bed was turned down neatly. The stair carpets were spotless as of old, and the furniture and banisters shone. Winnie conducted a further brief altercation in the kitchen and then was quiet till tea when my mother went to bed and so did she. I had a comfortable night. In the morning Winnie started fighting with herself again, or so it seemed. On investigation, I found her smiling while she argued. My mother's breakfast tray was all prepared and Winnie was about to carry it up to Ma's room. "What's the matter Winnie?" I said.

"Oh, the butter was forgot to be put on the tray. Too old for the job."

"Would you like to leave, Winnie?" I said,

somewhat desperately, but feeling that this was Winnie's way of saying just that.

"How could I leave your mother?" said Winnie, marching off with the tray.

Well, my mother, aged ninety-six, died suddenly during the following week. Winnie phoned me quite calmly from Sussex and I went down right away. There was a little quiet funeral. The house was to be sold. Winnie was still having occasional outbreaks against herself, such as "*The Times* didn't get cancelled at the newsagent like I said," and she muttered a bit as she went around. However, I spent a last, comfortable night in the house and after breakfast prepared to settle Winnie's pay and pension. I believed she would be glad of a rest. She had relations in Yorkshire and I thought she would probably want to return to them.

"I'm not leaving the family," said Winnie.

She didn't mean her family, she meant me.

"Well, Winnie, the house will be sold. There's no family left, is there?"

"I'm coming with you," Winnie said. "I've no doubt it's a pigsty but I can live in the basement."

My pigsty, my paradise. It was a small narrow house in a Hampstead lane, which I had acquired over twelve years ago. I never got round to putting it straight. It was so much my life to be out late at night at the theater, then usually some sort of supper after the theater with friends, in the morning doing my notes for the theater column, shuffling about in my dressing-gown; then after a quick lunch I would work in my study, or maybe go out to a cinema or an art show, or if not attend to something bureaucratic; or I would play some music on the piano. I worked hardest Fridays and Saturdays, for my last show was Friday and the column had to be in on Saturday at three in the afternoon. And since, until Ma died, I would go down to Sussex for Sunday and Monday with my friends, there was no time to put things straight. Sometimes there were people staying at my house and they would try to help. But it was better when they didn't for after one of those friendly tidy-ups I couldn't find anything. Never, on any occasion, did I allow anyone into my little study upstairs. A sullen and lady-like domestic help called Ida came mincing in three mornings a week for a couple of hours, painful all round, that is, to herself, to me and to my cat Francis. Ida took the clean dishes out of the dishwasher and stacked them away; she changed the towels and bed-sheets and left them at the laundry. She swept the kitchen floor, making short work of Francis with her broom, and sometimes she dusted the sitting-room and vacuumed the carpet. Francis cowered in the basement three mornings a week till she had gone.

It was not altogether the undesirability of Ida that persuaded me to take on Winnie. At first, I was decidedly dissuaded. The family fortunes had just managed to eke themselves out over my mother's lifetime. I am comfortably off, I have a job, but I'm by no means wealthy. Like most of my friends I wasn't in a position to take on a full-time housekeeper. And for another thing, I had no room. There was the damp basement full of rotting boxes which contained a great many other rotting objects that I always intended to do something about. These included some boxes of my mother's that had somehow landed at my house during one of her moves, and never been forwarded; once I had looked inside one of them; it had held two ostrich feather fans falling apart with moth, some carved wood chessmen the worse for the damp, some soggy books and some wine. On that occasion I threw back the contents into the box, less the wine which was still enjoyable. But I never again opened one of those boxes. The basement contained two rooms, a little dank bathroom and a frightful kitchen. It had plainly been inhabited before I acquired the house.

"I can't put you in the basement, Winnie," I said, instead of saying outright "I can't afford a cook-housekeeper, Winnie."

"What's wrong with the basement?"

"It's damp."

"I don't need much money," said Winnie. "Your mother underpaid me, anyway. Old-fashioned ideas. You need me to cook for you. I can go into the attic and make it over for a room."

How she knew about the attic I don't know. I had once thought of making it into a one-room apartment and renting it, but it was just above the two bedrooms of the house, one of which was my study, and I hadn't liked the thought of people moving about over my head. So the attic was empty. The other rooms in my house apart from my bedroom and my study were on the ground floor, a sitting room and a dining room with a divan where I put up occasional friends. The only place for Winnie was the attic, warm and empty. What made me waver in my resolve not to take on Winnie was that remark of hers, "You need me to cook for you." That was indeed a temptation. I visualized the effortless and good little supper parties I could give after the theater. The nice lunches I would have, always so well-planned, well-served; and Winnie was a very economical shopper.

"Save you a fortune in restaurants," decided Winnie; for it really was all decided. "And with the sale of your mother's house, you'll be in clover."

I didn't go into the fact that death duties were

taking care of my late mother's property, she having stubbornly arranged her affairs so badly. But it was true that restaurant-eating in London was becoming more and more difficult as the food and service were ever more inferior. I just said, "Well, Winnie, you'll have to settle yourself in the attic as best you can. I'll help you up with your things but beyond that, I'm a busy man."

"I haven't many things," Winnie said.

When she saw my house she said, "The Slough of Despond, if you remember your Bunyan." Nevertheless she settled into the attic. I paid off Ida and from then on was in Winnie's hands.

It was true my life was transformed. It was amazing what Winnie could do. Except for the study which I locked up every time I left the house and where Winnie could not penetrate, she penetrated everywhere. A new kitchen stove was her only extravagance. I paid no attention to Winnie's comings and goings but it was truly remarkable how she managed to clean out the house from the basement to the attic so well that I saw through the sitting-room windows as it seemed for the first time, and my bed was actually made every day. Winnie achieved all this in a very short time. Within a week I began to have friends to meals, delicious, interesting, just right.

"How lucky you are!" was what I heard from one friend after another. There were few who would not willingly have taken Winnie away from me if they'd had the chance. My mother's silver and crystal sparkled on the table. Winnie was quite up to serving at a late hour. And her meals were always marvellous. "Oh what elegance! How does she manage it?"

"Who is she arguing with, there in the kitchen?"

"Herself."

For one could hear Winnie, after she had cleared away and served us coffee, muttering to herself meanwhile, in the sitting room, still fighting her lonely battles in the kitchen.

I am a man of the theater, and this oddity of Winnie's certainly appealed to my sense of theater. Nor were my friends unappreciative of the carry-on. They thought it was delightful. As soon as she had left the room they called her a joy and they called her a treasure. One of my younger friends, an actress who had formerly liked to visit my mother in the country, had the quick eye to notice, what I hadn't noticed, that a couple of my chairs had been newly upholstered in genuine petit-point.

"You've had your mother's petit-point finished," she said. "I remember she was working on it all last summer. The last time I saw her just before she died she was sitting out on the terrace working at this."

"How do you know it's Ma's work?" I said.

"I recognize the pattern, look, that's the Venetian design, she had it done specially, look at that red."

"Well she must have finished it."

"Oh, that's impossible. It's very slow work. For your mother, impossible."

"Well, Winnie must have finished it."

"Winnie? How could she have managed it with all the other things she had to do?"

"One never knows what Winnie's up to."

I was suspicious. But, looking back on it, I think that the truth is I didn't want to know how Winnie did it. It was like admitting you didn't believe in Santa Claus: all those lovely surprises might stop.

Winnie's success with my friends wasn't lost on her. She, too, developed a sense of her theatrical side, muttering ever the more as she served the vegetables or the coffee; and one evening when I had a few guests, for no apparent reason she entered the room with one of my mother's mothy great ostrich feather fans in her hand and gave a performance of a pre-war debutante being presented at court, sweeping the fan before her and curtseying low, with the feathers flying all over the carpet. She solemnly left the room, backwards, treating us to another low genuflection before she left. Nobody spoke till she had gone, but Winnie's dottiness occupied the conversation merrily for the rest of the evening; secretly, I was a little embarrassed. Another time I was having a quiet game of chess with a friend when Winnie came in unnecessarily to tidy the fire. She had cleaned up those old chess pieces from Ma's trunk, they were positively a work of restoration. As she passed us she cast an eye at the board and said, "Undemocratic." I suppose she was referring to the kings and castles. But where Winnie was getting beyond a joke was on those days when, after lunch, I sat in my study trying to compose my theater column.

Winnie at that time of day was usually up in her room in the attic wildly remonstrating with herself. I could get no peace. Finally and reluctantly I had it out with her.

"Winnie," I said, very tactfully, "you're beginning to talk to yourself, you know. There's nothing to worry about, many people do it, in fact there are great geniuses who go about talking to themselves. It's only that I can't get on with my work when I hear these arguments going on over my head."

"Well, I'm much provoked," Winnie said.

"I've no doubt of that, and I think you really

do too much for me. Will you agree to see a doctor?"

"In an institution?" Winnie wanted to know.

"Oh, Winnie, of course not. Only privately. Maybe you need some medicine. Otherwise, I'm afraid we'll have to part. But I do urge you—"

I urged her into going to a young psychiatrist I'd heard of, in private practice. I have no idea what account she gave of herself and her condition but I've no doubt he got some illogical story out of her. She didn't appear to think there was anything wrong with her, and neither, apparently, did he. She refused to go into hospital under observation and he sent her away after a few visits with some medicine. I made enquires of the doctor but he wouldn't say much. "She has a few hallucinations, nothing to worry about. She should get over it. Of course I can't diagnose in depth without her coop- eration in a clinic." I settled his exorbitant bill. Winnie carried on in much the same way as before for about a week. She told me she was taking the medicine.

Then she did get quieter. Within two weeks she had stopped her racketing and shouting. I was able to get on with my work.

But slowly the house degenerated. It was like old times, only worse, because, although I began to eat out, Winnie burnt the food she prepared for herself. There was a super-chaos, a smell of burning and old rubbish all over the house. She bustled about brightly enough, but simply couldn't manage.

"Perhaps you need a holiday, Winnie."

"I stopped taking them pills," she said. "Rose didn't like them. They had an effect."

"Rose?"

"Rose Spigot."

I remember Miss Spigot, the cook who died. I remembered Miss Spigot with her specially careful enunciation, her prim and well-trained ways, and how she was said to have traveled with a duke's family all over the Orient. "Are you talking about some relation of our late cook?" I said.

"I'm talking about our late cook herself," said Winnie. "She's gone away. When I started to take the pills they put her off her stroke."

"By no means," I said wildly, "take anything whatsoever that doesn't suit you, Winnie."

"It's not me, it's Rose. She was a very provoking woman, acting the lady with your mother's needlework and objecting to me showing off in front of company. But she was a good cook-housekeeper, she's a good manager, and I can't cope alone with all the mess. She was another pair of hands."

"Definitely, you should stop the pills," I said. "Wouldn't you like me to have another word with the doctor?"

"Certainly not," said Winnie. "There was nothing wrong with the doctor."

I had to go away for a week to a theater festival in the north. I was glad to go, notwithstanding my crumpled shirts and unwashed socks crammed into my bag. I felt I could face the problem of Winnie better after a break.

When I got back, as I put my key in the door, I knew something had happened by the fact that my old brass name-plate was twinkling and by the sound of Winnie's voice from the back of the house raised in argument.

Only Winnie was in the kitchen when I put my head round the door. "Rose is back," said Winnie.

I could see what she meant. The house was clean and shining; my supper that night was excellent.

But it was all too much for my no doubt weak character. I thought it over for a bit and finally persuaded Winnie to retire. She went back to Yorkshire, accompanied by Miss Spigot or not I don't know. My house is the pigsty of old. My friends are awfully good to me and I dine out a lot.

The stuff that used to moulder in the basement is now rotting in the attic. Nobody combs Francis the cat, but he doesn't mind. When I'm on my own I can always sit down among the dust and the litter, and play the piano.

THE EXECUTOR

WHEN MY UNCLE DIED all the literary manuscripts went to a university foundation, except one. The correspondence went too, and the whole of his library. They came (a white-haired man and a young girl) and surveyed his study. Everything, they said, would be desirable and it would make a good price if I let the whole room go—his chair, his desk, the carpet, even his ashtrays. I agreed to this. I left everything in the drawers of the desk just as it was when my uncle died, including the bottle of Librium and a rusty razor blade.

My uncle died this way: he was sitting on the bank of the river, playing a fish. As the afternoon faded a man passed by, and then a young couple who made pottery passed him. As they said later, he was sitting peacefully awaiting the catch and of course they didn't disturb him. As night fell the colonel and his wife passed by; they were on their way home from their daily walk. They knew it was too late for my uncle to be simply sitting there, so they went to look. He had been dead, the doctor pronounced, from two to two and a half hours. The fish was still struggling with the bait. It was a mild heart attack. Everything my uncle did was mild, so different from everything he wrote. Yet perhaps not so different. He was supposed to be "far out," so one didn't know what went on out there. Besides, he had not long returned from a trip to London. They say, still waters run deep.

But far out was how he saw himself. He once said that if you could imagine modern literature as a painting, perhaps by Brueghel the Elder, the people and the action were in the foreground, full of color, eating, stealing, copulating, laughing, courting each other, excreting, and stabbing each other, selling things, climbing trees. Then in the distance, at the far end of a vast plain, there he would be, a speck on the horizon, always receding and always there, and always a necessary and mysterious component of the picture; always there and never to be taken away, essential to the picture—a speck in the distance, which if you were to blow up the detail would simply be a vague figure, plodding on the other way.

I am no fool, and he knew it. He didn't know it at first, but he had seven months in which to learn that fact. I gave up my job in Edinburgh in the government office, a job with a pension, to come here to the lonely house among the Pentland Hills to live with him and take care of things. I think he imagined I was going to be another Elaine when he suggested the arrangement. He had no idea how much better I was for him than Elaine. Elaine was his mistress, that is the stark truth. "My common-law wife," he called her, explaining that in Scotland, by tradition, the woman you are living with is your wife. As if I didn't know all that nineteenth-century folklore; and it's long died out. Nowadays you have to do more than say "I marry you, I marry you, I marry you," to make a woman your wife. Of course, my uncle was a genius and a character. I allowed for that. Anyway, Elaine died and I came here a month later. Within a month I had cleared up the best part of the disorder. He called me a Scottish puritan girl, and at forty-one it was nice to be a girl and I wasn't against the Scottish puritanical attribution either since I am proud to be a Scot; I feel nationalistic about it. He always had that smile of his when he said it, so I don't know how he meant it. They say he had that smile of his when he was found dead, fishing.

"I appoint my niece Susan Kyle to be my sole literary executor." I don't wonder he decided on this course after I had been with him for three months. Probably for the first time in his life all his papers were in order. I went into Edinburgh and bought box-files and cover-files and I filed away all that mountain of papers, each under its separate heading. And I knew what was what. You didn't catch me filing away a letter from Angus Wilson or Saul Bellow in the same place as an ordinary "W" or "B," a Miss Mary Whitelaw or a Mrs. Jonathan Brown. I knew the value of these letters, they went into a famous-persons file, bulging and of value. So that in a short time my uncle said, "There's little for me to do now, Susan, but die." Which I thought was melodramatic, and said so. But I could see he was forced to admire my good sense. He said, "You remind me of my mother, who prepared her shroud all ready for her funeral." His mother was my grandmother Janet Kyle. Why shouldn't she have sat and sewn her shroud? People in those days had very little to do, and here I was running the house and looking after my uncle's papers with only the help of

Mrs. Donaldson three mornings a week, where my grandmother had four pairs of hands for indoor help and three out. The rest of the family never went near the house after my grandmother died, for Elaine was always there with my uncle.

The property was distributed among the family, but I was the sole literary executor. And it was up to me to do what I liked with his literary remains. It was a good thing I had everything inventoried and filed, ready for sale. They came and took the total archive as they called it away, all the correspondence and manuscripts except one. That one I kept for myself. It was the novel he was writing when he died, an unfinished manuscript. I thought, Why not? Maybe I will finish it myself and publish it. I am no fool, and my uncle must have known how the book was going to end. I never read any of his correspondence, mind you; I was too busy those months filing it all in order. I did think, however, that I would read this manuscript and perhaps put an ending to it. There were already ten chapters. My uncle had told me there was only another chapter to go. So I said nothing to the Foundation about that one unfinished manuscript; I was only too glad when they had come and gone, and the papers were out of the house. I got the painters in to clean the study. Mrs. Donaldson said she had never seen the house looking so like a house should be.

Under my uncle's will I inherited the house, and I planned eventually to rent rooms to tourists in the summer, bed and breakfast. In the meantime I set about reading the unfinished manuscript, for it was only April, and I'm not a one to let the grass grow under my feet. I had learned to decipher that old-fashioned handwriting of his which looked good on the page but was not too clear. My uncle had a treasure in me those last months of his life, although he said I was like a book without an index—all information, and no way of getting at it. I asked him to tell me what information he ever got out of Elaine, who never passed an exam in her life.

This last work of my uncle's was an unusual story for him, set in the seventeenth century here among the Pentland Hills. He had told me only that he was writing something strong and cruel, and that this was easier to accomplish in a historical novel. It was about the slow identification and final trapping of a witch, and I could see as I read it that he hadn't been joking when he said it was strong and cruel; he had often said things to frighten and alarm me, I don't know why. By chapter ten the trial of the witch in Edinburgh was only halfway through. Her fate depended entirely on chapter eleven, and on the negotiations that were being conducted behind the scenes by the opposing factions of intrigue. My uncle had left a pile of notes he had accumulated toward this novel, and I retained these along with the manuscript. But there was no sign in the notes as to how my uncle had decided to resolve the fate of the witch—whose name was Edith but that is by the way. I put the notebooks and papers away, for there were many other things to be done following the death of my famous uncle. The novel itself was written by hand in twelve notebooks. In the twelfth only the first two pages had been filled, the rest of the pages were blank; I am sure of this. The two filled pages came to the end of chapter ten. At the top of the next page was written "Chapter Eleven." I looked through the rest of the notebook to make sure my uncle had not made some note there on how he intended to continue; all blank, I am sure of it. I put the twelve notebooks, together with the sheaf of loose notes, in a drawer of the solid-mahogany dining-room sideboard.

A few weeks later I brought the notebooks out again, intending to consider how I might proceed with the completion of the book and so enhance its value. I read again through chapter ten; then, when I turned to the page where "Chapter Eleven" was written, there in my uncle's handwriting was the following:

Well, Susan, how do you feel about finishing my novel? Aren't you a greedy little snoot, holding back my unfinished work, when you know the Foundation paid for the lot? What about your puritanical principles? Elaine and I are waiting to see how you manage to write Chapter Eleven. Elaine asks me to add it's lovely to see you scouring and cleaning those neglected corners of the house. But don't you know, Jaimie is having you on. Where does he go after lunch?
—Your affec Uncle.

I could hardly believe my eyes. The first shock I got was the bit about Jaimie, and then came the second shock, that the words were there at all. It was twelve-thirty at night and Jaimie had gone home. Jaimie Donaldson is the son of Mrs. Donaldson, and it isn't his fault he's out of work. We have had experiences together, but nobody is to know that, least of all Mrs. Donaldson who introduced him into the household merely to clean the windows and stoke the boiler. But the words? Where did they come from?

It is a lonely house, here in a fold of the Pentlands, surrounded by woods, five miles to the nearest cottage, six to Mrs. Donaldson's, and the buses stop at ten p.m. I felt a great fear there in the dining-room, with the twelve notebooks on the table, and the pile of papers, a great cold, and a panic. I ran to the hall and lifted the telephone but didn't know how to explain myself or whom to phone. My story would sound like that of a woman gone crazy. Mrs. Donaldson? The police? I couldn't think what to say to them at that hour of night. "I have found some words that weren't there before in my uncle's manuscript, and in his own hand." It was unthinkable. Then I thought perhaps someone had played me a trick. Oh no, I knew that this couldn't be. Only Mrs. Donaldson had been in the dining-room, and only to dust, with me to help her. Jaimie had no chance to go there, not at all. I never used the dining-room now and had meals in the kitchen. But in fact I knew it wasn't them, it was Uncle. I wished with all my heart that I was a strong woman, as I had always felt I was, strong and sensible. I stood in the hall by the telephone, shaking. "O God, everlasting and almighty," I prayed, "make me strong, and guide and lead me as to how Mrs. Thatcher would conduct herself in circumstances of this nature."

I didn't sleep all night. I sat in the big kitchen stoking up the fire. Only once I moved, to go back into the dining-room and make sure that those words were there. Beyond a doubt they were, and in my uncle's handwriting—that handwriting it would take an expert forger to copy. I put the manuscript back in the drawer; I locked the dining-room door and took the key. My uncle's study, now absolutely empty, was above the kitchen. If he was haunting the house, I heard no sound from there or from anywhere else. It was a fearful night, waiting there by the fire.

Mrs. Donaldson arrived in the morning, complaining that Jaimie was getting lazy; he wouldn't rise. Too many late nights.

"Where does he go after lunch?" I said.

"Oh, he goes for a round of golf after his dinner," she said. "He's always ready for a round of golf no matter what else there is to do. Golf is the curse of Scotland."

I had a good idea who Jaimie was meeting on the golf course, and I could almost have been grateful to Uncle for pointing out to me in that sly way of his that Jaimie wandered in the hours after the mid-day meal which we called lunch and they called their dinner. By five o'clock in the afternoon Jaimie would come here to the house to fetch up the coal, bank the fire, and so forth. But all afternoon he would be on the links with that girl who works at the manse, Greta, younger sister of Elaine, the one who moved in here openly, ruining my uncle's morals, leaving the house to rot. I always suspected that family. After Elaine died it came out he had even introduced her to all his friends; I could tell from the letters of condolence, how they said things like "He never got over the loss of Elaine" and "He couldn't live without her." And sometimes he called me Elaine by mistake. I was furious. Once, for example, I said, "Uncle, stop pacing about down here. Go up to your study and do your scribbling; I'll bring you a cup of cocoa." He said with that glazed-eyed look he always had when he was interrupted in his thoughts, "What's come over you, Elaine?" I said, "I'm not Elaine, thank you very much." "Oh, of course," he said, "you are not Elaine, you are most certainly not her." If the public that read his book by the tens of thousands could have seen behind the scenes, I often wondered what they would have thought. I told him so many a time, but he smiled in that sly way, that smile he still had on his face when they found him fishing and stone dead.

After Mrs. Donaldson left the house, at noon, I went up to my bedroom, half dropping from lack of sleep. Mrs. Donaldson hadn't noticed anything; you could be falling down dead—they never look at you. I slept till four. It was still light. I got up and locked the doors, front and back. I pulled the curtains shut, and when Jaimie rang the bell at five o'clock I didn't open, I just let him ring. Eventually he went away. I expect he had plenty to wonder about. But I wasn't going to make him welcome before the fire and get him his supper, and take off my clothes there in the back room on the divan with him, in front of the television, while Uncle and Elaine were looking on, even though it is only Nature. No, I turned on the television for myself. You would never believe, it was a program on the Scottish BBC about Uncle. I switched to TV One, and got a quiz show. And I felt hungry, for I'd eaten nothing since the night before.

But I couldn't face any supper until I had assured myself about that manuscript. I was fairly certain by now that it was a dream. "Maybe I've been over-working," I thought to myself. I had the key of the dining-room in my pocket and I took it and opened the door; I closed the curtains, and I went to the drawer and took out the notebook.

Not only were the words that I had read last night there, new words were added, a whole paragraph:

Look up the Acts of the Apostles, Chapter 5, verses 1 to 10. See what happened to Ananias and Sapphira his wife. You're not getting on very fast with your scribbling, are you, Susan? Elaine and I were under the impression you were going to write

*Chapter Eleven. Why don't you take a cup of
cocoa and get on with it? First read Acts, V, 1–10.*
　　　　　　　　　　　　—Your affec Uncle.

Well, I shoved the book in the drawer and
looked round the dining-room. I looked under the
table and behind the curtains. It didn't look as if
anything had been touched. I got out of the room
and locked the door, I don't know how. I went to
fetch my Bible, praying, "O God omnipotent and
all-seeing, direct and instruct me as to the way out
of this situation, astonishing as it must appear to
Thee." I looked up the passage:

*But a certain man named Ananias, with Sap-
phira his wife, sold a possession.*

*And kept back part of the price, his wife also
being privy to it, and brought a certain part and
laid it at the apostles' feet.*

*But Peter said, Ananias, why hath Satan filled
thine heart to lie to the Holy Ghost, and to keep
back part of the land?*

I didn't read any more because I knew how it
went on. Ananias and Sapphira, his wife, were
both struck dead for holding back the portion of
the sale for themselves. This was Uncle getting at
me for holding back his manuscript from the

Foundation. That's an impudence, I thought, to make such a comparison from the Bible, when he was an open and avowed sinner himself.

I thought it all over for a while. Then I went into the dining-room and got out that last note-book. Something else had been written since I had put it away, not half an hour before:

Why don't you get on with Chapter Eleven? We're waiting for it.

I tore out the page, put the book away and locked the door. I took the page to the fire and put it on to burn. Then I went to bed.

This went on for a month. My uncle always started the page afresh with "Chapter Eleven," followed by a new message. He even went so far as to put in that I had kept back bits of the house-keeping money, although, he wrote, I was well paid enough. That's a matter of opinion, and who did the economising, anyway? Always, after reading Uncle's disrespectful comments, I burned the page, and we were getting near the end of the notebook. He would say things to show he followed me round the house, and even knew my dreams. When I went into Edinburgh for some shopping he knew exactly where I had been and what I'd bought. He and Elaine listened in to my conversations on the telephone if I rang up an old friend. I didn't let anyone in the house except Mrs. Donaldson. No more Jaimie. He even knew if I took a dose of salts and how long I had sat in the bathroom, the awful old man.

Mrs. Donaldson one morning said she was leaving. She said to me, "Why don't you see a doctor?" I said, "Why?" But she wouldn't speak.

One day soon afterwards a man rang me up from the Foundation. They didn't want to bother me, they said, but they were rather puzzled. They had found in Uncle's letters many references to a novel, *The Witch of the Pentlands*, which he had been writing just before his death; and they had found among the papers a final chapter to this novel, which he had evidently written on loose pages on a train, for a letter of his, kindly provided by one of his many correspondents, proved this. Only they had no idea where the rest of the manuscript could be. In the end the witch Edith is condemned to be burned, but dies of her own will power before the execution, he said, but there must be ten more chapters leading up to it. This was Uncle's most metaphysical work, and based on a true history, the man said, and he must stress that it was very important.

I said that I would have a look. I rang back that afternoon and said I had found the whole book in a drawer in the dining-room.

So the man came to get it. On the phone he sounded very suspicious, in case there were more manuscripts. "Are you sure that's everything? You know, the Foundation's price included the whole archive. No, don't trust it to the mail, I'll be there tomorrow at two."

Just before he arrived I took a good drink, whisky and soda, as, indeed, I had been taking from sheer need all the past month. I had brought out the notebooks. On the blank page was written:

Good-bye, Susan. It's lovely being a speck in the distance.

—Your affec Uncle.

THE PORTOBELLO
ROAD

ONE DAY IN MY young youth at high summer, lolling with my lovely companions upon a haystack, I found a needle. Already and privately for some years I had been guessing that I was set apart from the common run, but this of the needle attested the fact to my whole public: George, Kathleen and Skinny. I sucked my thumb, for when I had thrust my idle hand deep into the hay, the thumb was where the needle had struck.

When everyone had recovered George said, "She put in her thumb and pulled out a plum." Then away we were into our merciless hacking-hecking laughter again.

The needle had gone fairly deep into the thumby cushion and a small red river flowed and

spread from this tiny puncture. So that nothing of
our joy should lag, George put in quickly,

"Mind your bloody thumb on my shirt."

Then hac-hec-hoo, we shrieked into the hot
Borderland afternoon. Really I should not care to
be so young of heart again. That is my thought
every time I turn over my old papers and come
across the photograph. Skinny, Kathleen and myself are in the photo atop the haystack. Skinny had
just finished analysing the inwards of my find.

"It couldn't have been done by brains. You
haven't much brains but you're a lucky wee thing."

Everyone agreed that the needle betokened extraordinary luck. As it was becoming a serious
conversation, George said,

"I'll take a photo."

I wrapped my hanky round my thumb and got
myself organised. George pointed up from his
camera and shouted,

"Look, there's a mouse!"

Kathleen screamed and I screamed although I
think we knew there was no mouse. But this gave
us an extra session of squalling hee-hoo's. Finally
we three composed ourselves for George's picture.
We look lovely and it was a great day at the time,
but I would not care for it all over again. From
that day I was known as Needle.

• • •

One Saturday in recent years I was mooching down the Portobello Road, threading among the crowds of marketers on the narrow pavement when I saw a woman. She had a haggard, care-worn wealthy look, thin but for the breasts forced-up high like a pigeon's. I had not seen her for nearly five years. How changed she was! But I recognized Kathleen, my friend; her features had already begun to sink and protrude in the way that mouths and noses do in people destined always to be old for their years. When I had last seen her, nearly five years ago, Kathleen, barely thirty, had said,

"I've lost all my looks, it's in the family. All the women are handsome as girls, but we go off early, we go brown and nosey."

I stood silently among the people, watching. As you will see, I wasn't in a position to speak to Kathleen. I saw her shoving in her avid manner from stall to stall. She was always fond of antique jewelry and of bargains. I wondered that I had not seen her before in the Portobello Road on my Saturday morning ambles. Her long stiff-crooked fingers pounced to select a jade ring from among the jumble of brooches and pendants, onyx, moonstone and gold, set out on the stall.

"What do you think of this?" she said.

I saw then who was with her. I had been half-conscious of the huge man following several paces behind her, and now I noticed him.

"It looks all right," he said. "How much is it?"

"How much is it?" Kathleen asked the vendor.

I took a good look at this man accompanying Kathleen. It was her husband. The beard was unfamiliar, but I recognized beneath it his enormous mouth, the bright sensuous lips, the large brown eyes forever brimming with pathos.

It was not for me to speak to Kathleen, but I had a sudden inspiration which caused me to say quietly,

"Hallo, George."

The giant of a man turned round to face the direction of my face. There were so many people— but at length he saw me.

"Hallo, George," I said again.

Kathleen had started to haggle with the stall-owner, in her old way, over the price of the jade ring. George continued to stare at me, his big mouth slightly parted so that I could see a wide slit of red lips and white teeth between the fair grassy growths of beard and moustache.

"My God!" he said.

"What's the matter?" said Kathleen.

"Hallo, George!" I said again, quite loud this time, and cheerfully.

"Look!" said George. "Look who's there, over beside the fruit stall."

Kathleen looked but didn't see.

"Who is it?" she said impatiently.

"It's Needle," he said. "She said 'Hallo, George.'"

"*Needle*," said Kathleen. "Who do you mean? You don't mean our old friend *Needle* who—"

"Yes. There she is. My God!"

He looked very ill, although when I had said "Hallo, George" I had spoken friendly enough.

"I don't see anyone faintly resembling poor Needle," said Kathleen looking at him. She was worried.

George pointed straight at me. "Look *there*. I tell you that is Needle."

"You're ill, George. Heavens, you must be seeing things. Come on home. Needle isn't there. You know as well as I do, Needle is dead."

I must explain that I departed this life nearly five years ago. But I did not altogether depart this world. There were those odd things still to be done which one's executors can never do properly. Papers to be looked over, even after the executors have torn them up. Lots of business except, of course, on Sundays and Holidays of Obligation, plenty to take an interest in for the time being. I take my recreation on Saturday mornings. If it is a wet Saturday I wander up and down the substantial lanes of Woolworth's as I did when I was young and visible. There is a pleasurable spread of objects on the counters which I now perceive and exploit with a certain detachment, since it suits with my condition of life. Creams, toothpastes, combs and hankies, cotton gloves, flimsy flowering scarves, writing-paper and crayons, ice-cream cones and orangeade, screwdrivers, boxes of tacks, tins of paint, of glue, of marmalade; I always liked them but far more now that I have no need of any. When Saturdays are fine I go instead to the Portobello Road where formerly I would jaunt with Kathleen in our grown-up days. The barrow-loads do not change much, of apples and rayon vests in common blues and low-taste mauve, of silver plate, trays and teapots long since changed hands from the bygone citizens to dealers, from shops to the new flats and breakable homes, and then over to the barrow-stalls and the dealers again: Georgian spoons, rings, earrings of turquoise and opal set in the butterfly pattern of true-lovers' knot, patch-boxes with miniature paintings of ladies on ivory, snuff-boxes of silver with Scotch pebbles inset.

Sometimes as occasion arises on a Saturday

morning, my friend Kathleen, who is a Catholic, has a Mass said for my soul, and then I am in attendance, as it were, at the church. But most Saturdays I take my delight among the solemn crowds with their aimless purposes, their eternal life not far away, who push past the counters and stalls, who handle, buy, steal, touch, desire and ogle the merchandise. I hear the tinkling tills, I hear the jangle of loose change and tongues and children wanting to hold and have.

That is how I came to be in the Portobello Road that Saturday morning when I saw George and Kathleen. I would not have spoken had I not been inspired to it. Indeed it's one of the things I can't do now—to speak out, unless inspired. And most extraordinary, on that morning as I spoke, a degree of visibility set in. I suppose from poor George's point of view it was like seeing a ghost when he saw me standing by the fruit barrow repeating in so friendly a manner, "Hallo, George!"

We were bound for the south. When our education, what we could get of it from the north, was thought to be finished, one by one we were sent or sent for to London. John Skinner, whom we called Skinny, went to study more archaeology, George to join his uncle's tobacco farm, Kathleen to stay with her rich connections and to potter intermittently in the Mayfair hat shop which one of them owned. A little later I also went to London to see life, for it was my ambition to write about life, which first I had to see.

"We four must stick together," George said very often in that yearning way of his. He was always desperately afraid of neglect. We four looked likely to shift off in different directions and George did not trust the other three of us not to forget all about him. More and more as the time came for him to depart for his uncle's tobacco farm in Africa he said,

"We four must keep in touch."

And before he left he told each of us anxiously,

"I'll write regularly, once a month. We must keep together for the sake of the old times." He had had three prints taken from the negative of that photo on the haystack, wrote on the back of them "George took this the day that Needle found the needle" and gave us a copy each. I think we all wished he could become a bit more callous.

During my lifetime I was a drifter, nothing organised. It was difficult for my friends to follow the logic of my life. By the normal reckonings I should have come to starvation and ruin, which I never did. Of course, I did not live to write about life as I wanted to do. Possibly that is why I am inspired to do so now in these peculiar circumstances.

I taught in a private school in Kensington for almost three months, very small children. I didn't know what to do with them but I was kept fairly busy escorting incontinent little boys to the lavatory and telling the little girls to use their handkerchiefs. After that I lived a winter holiday in London on my small capital, and when that had run out I found a diamond bracelet in the cinema for which I received a reward of fifty pounds. When it was used up I got a job with a publicity man, writing speeches for absorbed industrialists, in which the dictionary of quotations came in very useful. So it went on. I got engaged to Skinny, but shortly after that I was left a small legacy, enough to keep me for six months. This somehow decided me that I didn't love Skinny so I gave him back the ring.

But it was through skinny that I went to Africa. He was engaged with a party of researchers to investigate King Solomon's mines, that series of ancient workings ranging from the ancient port of Ophir, now called Beira, across Portuguese East Africa and Southern Rhodesia to the mighty jungle-city of Zimbabwe whose temple walls still stand by the approach to an ancient and sacred mountain, where the rubble of that civilization scatters itself over the surrounding Rhodesian waste. I accompanied the party as a sort of secretary. Skinny vouched for me, he paid my fare, he sympathized by his action with my inconsequential life although when he spoke of it he disapproved. A life like mine annoys most people; they go to their jobs every day, attend to things, give orders, pummel typewriters, and get two or three weeks off every year, and it vexes them to see someone else not bothering to do these things and yet getting away with it, not starving, being lucky as they call it. Skinny, when I had broken off our engagement, lectured me about this, but still he took me to Africa knowing I should probably leave his unit within a few months.

We were there a few weeks before we began enquiring for George, who was farming about four hundred miles away to the north. We had not told him of our plans.

"If we tell George to expect us in his part of the world he'll come rushing to pester us the first week. After all, we're going on business," Skinny had said.

Before we left Kathleen told us, "Give George my love and tell him not to send frantic cables every time I don't answer his letters right away. Tell him I'm busy in the hat shop and being presented. You would think he hadn't another friend in the world the way he carries on."

We had settled first at Fort Victoria, our nearest place of access to the Zimbabwe ruins. There we made enquiries about George. It was clear he hadn't many friends. The older settlers were the most tolerant about the half-caste woman he was living with, as we found, but they were furious about his methods of raising tobacco which we learned were most unprofessional and in some mysterious way disloyal to the whites. We could never discover how it was that George's style of tobacco farming gave the blacks opinions about themselves, but that's what the older settlers claimed. The newer immigrants thought he was unsociable and, of course, his living with that nig made visiting impossible.

I must say I was myself a bit off-put by this news about the brown woman. I was brought up in a university town to which came Indian, African and Asiatic students in a variety of tints and hues. I was brought up to avoid them for reasons connected with local reputation and God's ordinances. You cannot easily go against what you were brought up to do unless you are a rebel by nature.

Anyhow, we visited George eventually, taking advantage of the offer of transport from some people bound north in search of game. He had heard of our arrival in Rhodesia and though he was glad, almost relieved, to see us he pursued a policy of sullenness for the first hour.

"We wanted to give you a surprise, George."

"How were we to know that you'd get to hear of our arrival, George? News here must travel faster than light, George."

"We did hope to give you a surprise, George."

At last he said, "Well, I must say it's good to see you. All we need now is Kathleen. We four simply must stick together. You find when you're in a place like this, there's nothing like old friends."

He showed us his drying sheds. He showed us a paddock where he was experimenting with a horse and a zebra mare, attempting to mate them. They were frolicking happily, but not together. They passed each other in their private play time and again, but without acknowledgment and without resentment.

"It's been done before," George said. "It makes a fine strong beast, more intelligent than a mule and sturdier than a horse. But I'm not having any success with this pair, they won't look at each other."

After a while, he said, "Come in for a drink and meet Matilda."

She was dark brown, with a subservient hollow chest and round shoulders, a gawky woman, very snappy with the house-boys. We said pleasant things as we drank on the porch before dinner, but

we found George difficult. For some reason he
began to rail at me for breaking off my engagement to Skinny, saying what a dirty trick it was
after all those good times in the old days. I di-
verted attention to Matilda. I supposed, I said, she
knew this part of the country well?

"No," said she, "I been a-shellitered my life. I
not put out to working. Me nothing to go from
place to place is allowed like dirty girls does." In
her speech she gave every syllable equal stress.

George explained, "Her father was a white
magistrate in Natal. She had a sheltered upbringing, different from the other coloreds, you realize."

"Man, me no black-eyed Susan," said Matilda,
"no, no."

On the whole, George treated her as a servant.
She was about four months advanced in preg-
nancy, but he made her get up and fetch for him,
many times. Soap: that was one of the things
Matilda had to fetch. George made his own bath
soap, showed it proudly, gave us the recipe which I
did not trouble to remember; I was fond of nice
soaps during my lifetime and George's smelt of
brilliantine and looked likely to soil one's skin.

"D'yo brahn?" Matilda asked me.

George said, "She is asking if you brown in the
sun."

"No, I go freckled."

"I got sister-in-law go freckles."

She never spoke another word to Skinny nor to me, and we never saw her again.

Some months later I said to Skinny,

"I'm fed up with being a camp-follower."

He was not surprised that I was leaving his unit, but he hated my way of expressing it. He gave me a Presbyterian look.

"Don't talk like that. Are you going back to England or staying?"

"Staying, for a while."

"Well, don't wander too far off."

I was able to live on the fee I got for writing a gossip column in a local weekly, which wasn't my idea of writing about life, of course. I made friends, more than I could cope with, after I left Skinny's exclusive little band of archaeologists. I had the attractions of being newly out from England and of wanting to see life. Of the countless young men and go-ahead families who purred me along the Rhodesian roads, hundred after hundred miles, I only kept up with one family when I returned to my native land. I think that was because they were the most representative, they stood for all the rest: people in those parts are very typical of each other, as one group of standing stones in that wilderness is like the next.

I met George once more in a hotel in Bulawayo. We drank highballs and spoke of war. Skinny's party were just then deciding whether to remain in the country or return home. They had reached an exciting part of their research, and whenever I got a chance to visit Zimbabwe he would take me for a moonlight walk in the ruined temple and try to make me see phantom Phoenicians flitting ahead of us, or along the walls. I had half a mind to marry Skinny; perhaps, I thought, when his studies were finished. The impending war was in our bones: so I remarked to George as we sat drinking highballs on the hotel porch in the hard bright sunny July winter of that year.

George was inquisitive about my relations with Skinny. He tried to pump me for about half an hour and when at last I said, "You are becoming aggressive, George," he stopped. He became quite pathetic. He said, "War or no war I'm clearing out of this."

"It's the heat does it," I said.

"I'm clearing out in any case. I've lost a fortune in tobacco. My uncle is making a fuss. It's the other bloody planters; once you get the wrong side of them you're finished in this wide land."

"What about Matilda?" I asked.

He said, "She'll be all right. She's got hundreds of relatives."

I had already heard about the baby girl. Coal black, by repute, with George's features. And another on the way, they said.

"What about the child?"

He didn't say anything to that. He ordered more highballs and when they arrived he swizzled his for a long time with a stick. "Why didn't you ask me to your twenty-first?" he said then.

"I didn't have anything special, no party, George. We had a quiet drink among ourselves, George, just Skinny and the old professors and two of the wives and me, George."

"You didn't ask me to your twenty-first," he said. "Kathleen writes to me regularly."

This wasn't true. Kathleen sent me letters fairly often in which she said, "Don't tell George I wrote to you as he will be expecting word from me and I can't be bothered actually."

"But you," said George, "don't seem to have any sense of old friendship, you and Skinny."

"Oh, George!" I said.

"Remember the times we had," George said. "We used to have times." His large brown eyes began to water.

"I'll have to be getting along," I said.

"Please don't go. Don't leave me just yet. I've something to tell you."

"Something nice?" I laid on an eager smile. All responses to George had to be overdone.

"You don't know how lucky you are," George said.

"How?" I said. Sometimes I got tired of being called lucky by everybody. There were times when, privately practising my writings about life, I knew the bitter side of my fortune. When I failed again and again to reproduce life in some satisfactory and perfect form, I was the more imprisoned, for all my carefree living, within my craving for this satisfaction. Sometimes, in my impotence and need I secreted a venom which infected all my life for days on end and which spurted out indiscriminately on Skinny or on anyone who crossed my path.

"You aren't bound by anyone," George said. "You come and go as you please. Something always turns up for you. You're free, and you don't know your luck."

"You're a damn sight more free than I am," I said sharply. "You've got your rich uncle."

"He's losing interest in me," George said. "He's had enough."

"Oh well, you're young yet. What was it you wanted to tell me?"

"A secret," George said. "Remember we used to have those secrets."

"Oh, yes we did."

"Did you ever tell any of mine?"

"Oh no, George" In reality, I couldn't remember any particular secret out of the dozens we must have exchanged from our schooldays onwards.

"Well, this is a secret, mind. Promise not to tell."

"Promise."

"I'm married."

"Married, George! Oh, who to?"

"Matilda."

"How dreadful!" I spoke before I could think, but he agreed with me.

"Yes, it's awful, but what could I do?"

"You might have asked my advice," I said pompously.

"I'm two years older than you are. I don't ask advice from you, Needle, little beast."

"Don't ask for sympathy then."

"A nice friend you are," he said, "I must say after all these years."

"Poor George!" I said.

"There are three white men to one white woman in this country," said George. "An isolated planter doesn't see a white woman and if he sees one she doesn't see him. What could I do? I needed the woman."

I was nearly sick. One, because of my Scottish upbringing. Two, because of my horror of corny phrases like "I needed the woman," which George repeated twice again.

"And Matilda got tough," said George, "after you and Skinny came to visit us. She had some friends at the Mission, and she packed up and went to them."

"You should have let her go," I said.

"I went after her," George said. "She insisted on being married, so I married her."

"That's not a proper secret, then," I said. "The news of a mixed marriage soon gets about."

"I took care of that," George said. "Crazy as I was, I took her to the Congo and married her there. She promised to keep quiet about it."

"Well, you can't clear off and leave her now, surely," I said.

"I'm going to get out of this place. I can't stand the woman and I can't stand the country. I didn't realize what it would be like. Two years of the country and three months of my wife has been enough."

"Will you get a divorce?"

"No, Matilda's Catholic. She won't divorce."

George was fairly getting through the high-balls, and I wasn't far behind him. His brown eyes floated shiny and liquid as he told me how he had written to tell his uncle of his plight, "Except, of course, I didn't say we were married, that would have been too much for him. He's a prejudiced hardened old colonial. I only said I'd had a child by a colored woman and was expecting another, and he perfectly understood. He came at once by plane a few weeks ago. He's made a settlement on her, providing she keeps her mouth shut about her association with me."

"Will she do that?"

"Oh, yes, or she won't get the money."

"But as your wife she has a claim on you, in any case."

"If she claimed as my wife she'd get far less. Matilda knows what she's doing, greedy bitch she is. She'll keep her mouth shut."

"Only, you won't be able to marry again, will you, George?"

"Not unless she dies," he said. "And she's as strong as a trek ox."

"Well, I'm sorry, George," I said.

"Good of you to say so," he said. "But I can see by your chin that you disapprove of me. Even my old uncle understood."

"Oh, George, I quite understand. You were lonely, I suppose."

"You didn't even ask me to your twenty-first. If you and Skinny had been nicer to me, I would never have lost my head and married the woman, never."

"You didn't ask me to your wedding," I said.

"You're a catty bissom, Needle, not like what you were in the old times when you used to tell us your wee stories."

"I'll have to be getting along," I said.

"Mind you keep the secret," George said.

"Can't I tell Skinny? He would be very sorry for you, George."

"You mustn't tell anyone. Keep it a secret. Promise."

"Promise," I said. I understood that he wished to enforce some sort of bond between us with this secret, and I thought, "Oh well, I suppose he's lonely. Keeping his secret won't do any harm."

I returned to England with Skinny's party just before the war.

I did not see George again till just before my death, five years ago.

After the war Skinny returned to his studies. He had two more exams, over a period of eighteen months, and I thought I might marry him when the exams were over.

"You might do worse than Skinny," Kathleen used to say to me on our Saturday morning excursions to the antique shops and the junk stalls.

She too was getting on in years. The remainder of our families in Scotland were hinting that it was time we settled down with husbands. Kathleen was a little younger than me, but looked much older. She knew her chances were diminishing but at that time I did not think she cared very much. As for myself, the main attraction of marrying Skinny was his prospective expeditions to Mesopotamia. My desire to marry him had to be stimulated by the continual reading of books about Babylon and Assyria; perhaps Skinny felt this, because he supplied the books and even started instructing me in the art of deciphering cuneiform tablets.

Kathleen was more interested in marriage than I thought. Like me, she had racketed around a good deal during the war; she had actually been engaged to an officer in the U.S. Navy, who was killed. Now she kept an antique shop near Lambeth, was doing very nicely, lived in a Chelsea square, but for all that she must have wanted to be married and have children. She would stop and look into all the prams which the mothers had left outside shops or area gates.

"The poet Swinburne used to do that," I told her once.

"Really? Did he want children of his own?"

"I shouldn't think so. He simply liked babies."

Before Skinny's final exam he fell ill and was sent to a sanatorium in Switzerland.

"You're fortunate after all not to be married to him," Kathleen said. "You might have caught T.B."

I was fortunate, I was lucky . . . so everyone kept telling me on different occasions. Although it annoyed me to hear, I knew they were right, but in a way that was different from what they meant. It took me very small effort to make a living; book reviews, odd jobs for Kathleen, a few months with the publicity man again, still getting up speeches about literature, art and life for industrial tycoons. I was waiting to write about life and it seemed to me that the good fortune lay in this, whenever it should be. And until then I was assured of my charmed life, the necessities of existence always coming my way and I with far more leisure than anyone else. I thought of my type of luck after I became a Catholic and was being confirmed. The Bishop touches the candidate on the cheek, a symbolic reminder of the sufferings a Christian is supposed to undertake. I thought, how lucky, what a feathery symbol to stand for the hellish violence of its true meaning.

I visited Skinny twice in the two years that he

was in the sanatorium. He was almost cured, and expected to be home within a few months. I told Kathleen after my last visit.

"Maybe I'll marry Skinny when he's well again."

"Make it definite, Needle, and not so much of the maybe. You don't know when you're well off," she said.

This was five years ago, in the last year of my life. Kathleen and I had become very close friends. We met several times each week, and after our Saturday morning excursions in the Portobello Road very often I would accompany Kathleen to her aunt's house in Kent for a long week-end.

One day in the June of that year I met Kathleen specially for lunch because she had phoned me to say she had news.

"Guess who came into the shop this afternoon," she said.

"Who?"

"George."

We had half imagined George was dead. We had received no letters in the past ten years. Early in the war we had heard rumors of his keeping a night club in Durban, but nothing after that. We could have made enquiries if we had felt moved to do so.

At one time, when we discussed him, Kathleen had said,

"I ought to get in touch with poor George. But then I think he would write back. He would demand a regular correspondence again."

"We four must stick together," I mimicked.

"I can visualize his reproachful limpid orbs," Kathleen said.

Skinny said, "He's probably gone native. With his coffee concubine and a dozen mahogany kids."

"Perhaps he's dead," Kathleen said.

I did not speak of George's marriage, nor of any of his confidences in the hotel at Bulawayo. As the years passed we ceased to mention him except in passing, as someone more or less dead so far as we were concerned.

Kathleen was excited about George's turning up. She had forgotten her impatience with him in former days; she said,

"It was so wonderful to see old George. He seems to need a friend, feels neglected, out of touch with things."

"He needs mothering, I suppose."

Kathleen didn't notice the malice. She declared, "That's exactly the case with George. It always has been, I can see it now."

She seemed ready to come to any rapid new and happy conclusion about George. In the course of the afternoon he had told her of his wartime night club in Durban, his game-shooting expeditions since. It was clear he had not mentioned Matilda. He had put on weight, Kathleen told me, but he could carry it.

I was curious to see this version of George, but I was leaving for Scotland next day and did not see him till September of that year, just before my death. While I was in Scotland I gathered from Kathleen's letters that she was seeing George very frequently, finding enjoyable company in him, looking after him. "You'll be surprised to see how he has developed." Apparently he would hang round Kathleen in her shop most days, "it makes him feel useful" as she maternally expressed it. He had an old relative in Kent whom he visited at week-ends; this old lady lived a few miles from Kathleen's aunt, which made it easy for them to travel down together on Saturdays, and go for long country walks.

"You'll see such a difference in George," Kathleen said on my return to London in September. I was to meet him that night, a Saturday. Kathleen's aunt was abroad, the maid on holiday, and I was to keep Kathleen company in the empty house.

George had left London for Kent a few days earlier. "He's actually helping with the harvest down there!" Kathleen told me lovingly.

Kathleen and I planned to travel down together, but on that Saturday she was unexpectedly delayed in London on some business. It was arranged that I should go ahead of her in the early afternoon to see to the provisions for our party; Kathleen had invited George to dinner at her aunt's house that night.

"I should be with you by seven," she said. "Sure you won't mind the empty house? I hate arriving at empty houses, myself."

I said no, I liked an empty house.

So I did, when I got there. I had never found the house more likeable. A large Georgian vicarage in about eight acres, most of the rooms shut and sheeted, there being only one servant. I discovered that I wouldn't need to go shopping, Kathleen's aunt had left many and delicate supplies with notes attached to them: "Eat this up please do, see also fridge" and "A treat for three hungry people see also 2 bttles beaune for yr party on back kn table." It was like a treasure hunt as I followed clue after clue through the cool silent domestic quarters. A house in which there are no people—but with all the signs of tenancy—can be a most tranquil good place. People take up space in a house out of proportion to their size. On my previous visits I had seen the rooms overflowing as it seemed, with Kathleen, her aunt, and the little fat maidservant; they were always on the move. As I wandered through that part of the house which was in use, opening windows to let in the pale yellow air of September, I was not conscious that I, Needle, was taking up any space at all, I might have been a ghost.

The only thing to be fetched was the milk. I waited till after four when the milking should be done, then set off for the farm which lay across two fields at the back of the orchard. There, when the byreman was handing me the bottle, I saw George.

"Hallo, George," I said.

"Needle! What are you doing here?" he said.

"Fetching milk," I said.

"So am I. Well, it's good to see you, I must say."

As we paid the farm-hand, George said, "I'll walk back with you part of the way. But I mustn't stop, my old cousin's without any milk for her tea. How's Kathleen?"

"She was kept in London. She's coming on later, about seven, she expects."

We had reached the end of the first field. George's way led to the left and on to the main road.

"We'll see you tonight, then?" I said.

"Yes, and talk about old times."

"Grand," I said.

But George got over the stile with me.

"Look here," he said. "I'd like to talk to you, Needle."

"We'll talk tonight, George. Better not keep your cousin waiting for the milk." I found myself speaking to him almost as if he were a child.

"No, I want to talk to you alone. This is a good opportunity."

We began to cross the second field. I had been hoping to have the house to myself for a couple more hours and I was rather petulant.

"See," he said suddenly, "that haystack."

"Yes," I said absently.

"Let's sit there and talk. I'd like to see you up on a haystack again. I still keep that photo. Remember that time when—"

"I found the needle," I said quickly, to get it over.

But I was glad to rest. The stack had been broken up, but we managed to find a nest in it. I buried my bottle of milk in the hay for coolness. George placed his carefully at the foot of the stack.

"My old cousin is terribly vague, poor soul. A bit hazy in her head. She hasn't the least sense of time. If I tell her I've only been gone ten minutes she'll believe it."

I giggled, and looked at him. His face had grown much larger, his lips full, wide and with a ripe color that is strange in a man. His brown eyes were abounding as before with some inarticulate plea.

"So you're going to marry Skinny after all these years?"

"I really don't know, George."

"You played him up properly."

"It isn't for you to judge. I have my own reasons for what I do."

"Don't get sharp," he said, "I was only funning." To prove it, he lifted a tuft of hay and brushed my face with it.

"D'you know," he said next, "I didn't think you and Skinny treated me very decently in Rhodesia."

"Well, we were busy, George. And we were younger then, we had a lot to do and see. After all, we could see you any other time, George."

"A touch of selfishness," he said.

"I'll have to be getting along, George." I made to get down from the stack.

He pulled me back. "Wait, I've got something to tell you."

"O.K., George, tell me."

"First promise not to tell Kathleen. She wants it kept a secret so that she can tell you herself."

"All right. Promise."

"I'm going to marry Kathleen."

"But you're already married."

Sometimes I heard news of Matilda from the one Rhodesian family with whom I still kept up. They referred to her as "George's Dark Lady" and of course they did not know he was married to her. She had apparently made a good thing out of George, they said, for she minced around all tarted up, never did a stroke of work and was always unsettling the respectable colored girls in their neighborhood. According to accounts, she was a living example of the folly of behaving as George did.

"I married Matilda in the Congo," George was saying.

"It would still be bigamy," I said.

He was furious when I used that word bigamy. He lifted a handful of hay as if he would throw it in my face, but controlling himself meanwhile he fanned it at me playfully.

"I'm not sure that the Congo marriage was valid," he continued. "Anyway, as far as I'm concerned, it isn't."

"You can't do a thing like that," I said.

"I need Kathleen. She's been decent to me. I think we were always meant for each other, me and Kathleen."

"I'll have to be going," I said.

But he put his knee over my ankles, so that I couldn't move. I sat still and gazed into space.

He tickled my face with a wisp of hay.

"Smile up, Needle," he said; "let's talk like old times."

"Well?"

"No one knows about my marriage to Matilda except you and me."

"And Matilda," I said.

"She'll hold her tongue so long as she gets her payments. My uncle left an annuity for the purpose, his lawyers see to it."

"Let me go, George."

"You promised to keep it a secret," he said, "you promised."

"Yes, I promised."

"And now that you're going to marry Skinny, we'll be properly coupled off as we should have been years ago. We should have been—but youth!—our youth got in the way, didn't it?"

"Life got in the way," I said.

"But everything's going to be all right now. You'll keep my secret, won't you? You promised." He had released my feet. I edged a little further from him.

I said, "If Kathleen intends to marry you, I shall tell her that you're already married."

"You wouldn't do a dirty trick like that, Needle? You're going to be happy with Skinny, you wouldn't stand in the way of my—"

"I must, Kathleen's my best friend," I said swiftly.

He looked as if he would murder me and he did. He stuffed hay into my mouth until it could hold no more, kneeling on my body to keep it still, holding both my wrists tight in his huge left hand. I saw the red full lines of his mouth and white slit of his teeth last thing on earth. Not another soul passed by as he pressed my body into the stack, as he made a deep nest for me, tearing up the hay to make a groove the length of my corpse, and finally pulling the warm dry stuff in a mound over this concealment, so natural-looking in a broken haystack. Then George climbed down, took up his bottle of milk and went his way. I suppose that was why he looked so unwell when I stood, nearly five years later, by the barrow in the Portobello Road and said in easy tones, "Hallo, George!"

The Haystack Murder was one of the notorious crimes of that year.

My friends said, "A girl who had everything to live for."

After a search that lasted twenty hours, when my body was found, the evening papers said. "'Needle' is found: in haystack!"

Kathleen, speaking from that Catholic point of

view which takes some getting used to, said, "She was at Confession only the day before she died— wasn't she lucky?"

The poor byre-hand who sold us the milk was grilled for hour after hour by the local police, and later by Scotland Yard. So was George. He admitted walking as far as the haystack with me, but he denied lingering there.

"You hadn't seen your friend for ten years?" the Inspector asked him.

"That's right," said George.

"And you didn't stop to have a chat?"

"No. We'd arranged to meet later at dinner. My cousin was waiting for the milk, I couldn't stop."

The old soul, his cousin, swore that he hadn't been gone more than ten minutes in all, and she believed it to the day of her death a few months later. There was the microscopic evidence of hay on George's jacket, of course, but the same evidence was on every man's jacket in the district that fine harvest year. Unfortunately, the byreman's hands were even brawnier and mightier than George's. The marks on my wrists had been done by such hands, so the laboratory charts indicated when my post-mortem was all completed. But the wrist-marks weren't enough to pin down the crime to either man. If I hadn't been wearing my long-sleeved cardigan, it was said, the bruises might have matched up properly with someone's fingers.

Kathleen, to prove that George had absolutely no motive, told the police that she was engaged to him. George thought this a little foolish. They checked up on his life in Africa, right back to his living with Matilda. But the marriage didn't come out—who would think of looking up registers in the Congo? Not that this would have proved any motive for murder. All the same, George was relieved when the enquiries were over without the marriage to Matilda being disclosed. He was able to have his nervous breakdown at the same time as Kathleen had hers, and they recovered together and got married, long after the police had shifted the enquiries to an Air Force camp five miles from Kathleen's aunt's home. Only a lot of excitement and drinks came of those investigations. The Haystack Murder was one of the unsolved crimes that year.

Shortly afterwards the byre-hand emigrated to Canada to start afresh, with the help of Skinny who felt sorry for him.

After seeing George taken away home by Kathleen that Saturday in the Portobello Road, I thought that perhaps I might be seeing more of him in similar circumstances. The next Saturday I looked out for him, and at last there he was, without Kathleen, half-worried, half-hopeful.

I dashed his hopes. I said, "Hallo, George!"

He looked in my direction, rooted in the midst of the flowing market-mongers in that convivial street. I thought to myself, "He looks as if he had a mouthful of hay." It was the new bristly maize-colored beard and moustache surrounding his great mouth which suggested the thought, gay and lyrical as life.

"Hallo, George!" I said again.

I might have been inspired to say more on that agreeable morning, but he didn't wait. He was away down a side street and along another street and down one more, zig-zag, as far and as devious as he could take himself from the Portobello Road.

Nevertheless he was back again next week. Poor Kathleen had brought him in her car. She left it at the top of the street, and got out with him, holding him tight by the arm. It grieved me to see Kathleen ignoring the spread of scintillations on the stalls. I had myself seen a charming Battersea box quite to her taste, also a pair of enamelled silver earrings. But she took no notice of these wares, clinging close to George, and poor Kathleen—I hate to say how she looked.

And George was haggard. His eyes seemed to have got smaller as if he had been recently in pain.

He advanced up the road with Kathleen on his arm, letting himself lurch from side to side with his wife bobbing beside him, as the crowds asserted their rights of way.

"Oh, George!" I said. "You don't look at all well, George."

"Look!" said George. "Over there by the hardware barrow. That's Needle."

Kathleen was crying. "Come back home, dear," she said.

"Oh, you don't look well, George!" I said.

They took him to a nursing home. He was fairly quiet, except on Saturday mornings when they had a hard time of it to keep him indoors and away from the Portobello Road.

But a couple of months later he did escape. It was a Monday.

They searched for him in the Portobello Road, but actually he had gone off to Kent to the village near the scene of the Haystack Murder. There he went to the police and gave himself up, but they could tell from the way he was talking that there was something wrong with the man.

"I saw Needle in the Portobello Road three Saturdays running," he explained, "and they put me in a private ward but I got away while the nurses were seeing to the new patient. You remember the murder of Needle—well, I did it. Now you know the truth, and that will keep bloody Needle's mouth shut."

Dozens of poor mad fellows confess to every murder. The police obtained an ambulance to take him back to the nursing home. He wasn't there long. Kathleen gave up her shop and devoted herself to looking after him at home. But she found that the Saturday mornings were a strain. He insisted on going to see me in the Portobello Road and would come back to insist that he'd murdered Needle. Once he tried to tell her something about Matilda, but Kathleen was so kind and solicitous, I don't think he had the courage to remember what he had to say.

Skinny had always been rather reserved with George since the murder. But he was kind to Kathleen. It was he who persuaded them to emigrate to Canada so that George should be well out of reach of the Portobello Road.

George has recovered somewhat in Canada but of course he will never be the old George again, as Kathleen writes to Skinny. "That Haystack tragedy did for George," she writes, "I feel sorrier for George sometimes than I am for poor Needle. But I do often have Masses said for Needle's soul."

I doubt if George will ever see me again in the Portobello Road. He broods much over the crumpled snapshot he took of us on the haystack. Kathleen does not like the photograph, I don't wonder. For my part, I consider it quite a jolly snap, but I don't think we were any of us so lovely as we look in it, gazing blatantly over the ripe cornfields, Skinny with his humorous expression, I secure in my difference from the rest, Kathleen with her head prettily perched on her hand, each reflecting fearlessly in the face of George's camera the glory of the world, as if it would never pass.